"I think…I think I need some fresh air."

They abandoned the floor midsong, and Sierra made a beeline toward the exit. Outside, the night air was cool against her skin, but the second she looked into Jarrett's eyes, she was feverish again.

He spoke first. "I hope I didn't upset you with what I said."

"No. I'm glad you showed up here. Glad I got to dance with you."

"We don't have to stop," he said, pulling her closer.

"But maybe we should." Despite her sensible words, she leaned into him, indulging herself in the feel of their bodies tangled together. Her hands glided up his back. This was such a bad idea. "I work for you. My professionalism is very important to me." She was beginning to realize her job was all she had. "I would never compromise myself with a patient."

He brushed his thumb over the corner of her mouth, and she shivered. "Then I guess," he said as he lowered his head, "it's a good thing I'm not your patient."

Dear Reader,

One of my favorite things to do as a writer is revisit communities (like Cupid's Bow) and characters that I've already created. It's like spending time with old friends.

Physical therapist Sierra Bailey started out as a minor character in my 2014 book *The Texan's Christmas*. She was only in a few scenes, but I loved her feisty spirit. She proved to be the perfect heroine for this book, helping to heal not only her teenage patient, Vicki, but Vicki's older brother, guilt-stricken rancher Jarrett Ross.

Up until a few months ago, Jarrett lived an adrenaline-fueled existence that centered around rodeo wins and pretty women. But when he stood his sister up for dinner and she was in a horrible car accident, Jarrett came home to help take care of her and the family ranch. He's sworn off dating for the moment, and no woman is more off-limits than the beautiful physical therapist spending the month with them. Yet Sierra's determination, humor and heart are even more irresistible than her red hair and gorgeous curves.

Jarrett can't stop himself from falling for Sierra, but can he convince the woman who's only here on temporary assignment that her future could be in Cupid's Bow... with him?

This is the second installment in my Cupid's Bow, Texas series, and I hope you'll follow me on Twitter, @tanyamichaels, or Facebook (authortanyamichaels) to learn about my future Cupid's Bow books.

Happy reading,

Tanya

FALLING FOR
THE RANCHER

———

Tanya Michaels

HARLEQUIN® AMERICAN ROMANCE®

Recycling programs
for this product may
not exist in your area.

ISBN-13: 978-0-373-75614-8

Falling for the Rancher

Printed in U.S.A.

Tanya Michaels, a *New York Times* bestselling author and five-time RITA® Award nominee, has been writing love stories since middle school algebra class (which probably explains her math grades). Her books, praised for their poignancy and humor, have received awards from readers and reviewers alike. Tanya is an active member of Romance Writers of America and a frequent public speaker. She lives outside Atlanta with her very supportive husband, two highly imaginative kids and a bichon frise who thinks she's the center of the universe.

Books by Tanya Michaels

Harlequin American Romance

The Best Man in Texas
Texas Baby
His Valentine Surprise
A Mother's Homecoming
My Cowboy Valentine
"Hill Country Cupid"

Hill Country Heroes

Claimed by a Cowboy
Tamed by a Texan
Rescued by a Ranger

The Colorado Cades

Her Secret, His Baby
Second Chance Christmas
Her Cowboy Hero

Texas Rodeo Barons

The Texan's Christmas

Cupid's Bow, Texas

Falling for the Sheriff

All backlist available in ebook format.

Visit the Author Profile page
at Harlequin.com for more titles.

While I was writing this book that features someone in health care, my daughter actually had quite a few medical appointments. Thank you to her nurses—and nurses in general—for their time and effort in a demanding profession.

Chapter One

It was surreal, staring at a photo of himself and feeling as if he were looking at a stranger. No, that wasn't exactly right, Jarrett Ross amended, studying the framed rodeo picture on the wall of his father's home office. The word *stranger* implied he didn't know the dark-haired cowboy, that he had no feelings about him one way or the other.

A wave of contempt hit him as he studied the cocky smile and silvery, carefree gaze. *Selfish SOB.* Six months ago, his only concerns had been which events to ride and which appreciative buckle-bunny to celebrate with after he won. A lot had changed since then.

Six months ago, Vicki wasn't in a wheelchair.

"Jarrett?"

He turned as Anne Ross entered the room. He'd been so mired in regret he'd almost forgotten he was waiting for his mother. Dread welled as she closed the door behind her. Did they need the privacy because there was more bad news to discuss? He wanted to sink into the leather chair behind the desk and bury his face in his hands. But he remained standing, braced for whatever life threw at them next.

"How did Dad's appointment go?" Jarrett hadn't

been able to accompany his parents to the hospital this afternoon. There was too much to do at the Twisted R now that he was the only one working the ranch. But even without the countless tasks necessary to keep the place running, he would have stayed behind in case Vicki needed him—not that his sister voluntarily sought out his company these days.

"You know your father. He's a terrible patient." Anne rolled her eyes, but her attempt to lighten the situation didn't mask her concern. "Overall, the doctor says we're lucky. He's recovering as well as can be expected from the heart attack and the surgery. The thing is…"

Jarrett gripped the back of the chair, waiting for the other boot to drop.

His mother came forward and sat down in the chair across from him, the stress of the past few months plain on her face. Even more telling was the slump of her shoulders. She'd always had a ramrod-straight posture, whether sitting in a saddle or waltzing across a dance floor with her husband.

"I have to get your father off this ranch," she said bluntly. "I've been after him for years to slow down, to get away for a few days. I even tried to talk him into selling the place."

That revelation stunned Jarrett. He'd never realized his mom's complaints about the demands of ranch life were serious. He'd thought her occasional grumbling was generic and innocuous, like jokes about hating Mondays. People griped about it all the time, but no one actually suggested removing Monday from the calendar. It was impossible to imagine Gavin Ross anywhere but at the Twisted R. Not sure how to respond, he paced restlessly around the office. Despite the many hours he'd spent here over the past month, it still felt like trespassing. As if his father should be the one sitting behind the desk making the decisions that would affect the family.

"Your dad refuses to accept that he's not in his twenties anymore," his mom continued. "At the rate he's going, he'll work himself to death! And after the added stress of Vicki's accident…"

Guilt sliced through him. Was his dad's heart attack one more thing to trace back to that night in July? His mind echoed with the metallic jangling of the keys he'd tossed to his younger sister. He hadn't gone with her because a blonde named Tammy—or Taylor?— had been whispering in his ear, saying that as impressive as he'd been in eight seconds, she couldn't wait to see what magic he could work in an hour's time.

Jarrett pushed away the shameful memory. "So you and Dad want to take a few days of vacation?" he asked, leaning against the corner of the desk closest to her.

"A few weeks, actually. I haven't discussed it with him yet, but Dr. Wayne agrees that it's a good idea. My cousin has a very nice cabin near Lake Tahoe that she's been offering to let us use for years, and Dr. Wayne said he could give us the name of a good cardiologist in the area. Just in case."

When you were recovering from open-heart surgery, "just in case" wasn't nearly as casual as it sounded.

"Your father is mule-headed. Now that he's starting to feel a little better, he'll try to return to his usual workload. I can't let him do that. He may seem larger than life, but he's not invincible." Her gaze shifted downward. "And...without us as a buffer, Vicki would naturally turn to you for company and assistance."

The soft words were like a pitchfork to the gut. His sister, younger than him by almost seven years, had grown up idolizing Jarrett. Now his parents had to evacuate Texas just to force her to speak to him again.

"She's going to forgive you." Anne reached over to clasp his hand. "The drunk driver who plowed into the truck is to blame, not you."

He wanted to believe her, but it was his fault Vicki had been on the road. They'd had plans to grab a late dinner. Between his travel on the rodeo circuit and her being away for her freshman year of college, they'd barely seen each other since Christmas. But instead of catching up with his kid sister as promised, he'd ditched her in favor of getting laid. Vicki had been trapped amid twisted metal and broken glass when she should have been sitting in some restaurant booth, debating between chicken-fried steak and a rack of ribs. She'd always had a Texas-sized appetite, but her athletic hobbies kept her trim and fit.

Past tense. She no longer had much of an appetite. And although the doctors assured her that, with physical therapy, she would walk again, it would be a long damn time before she played softball or went to a dance club with her sorority sisters. She hadn't even been able to return to campus for the start of the new semester in August, another consequence that ate at him. Unlike Jarrett, who'd earned a degree with a combination of community-college courses and online classes, Vicki had been accepted into one of the best universities in the state. How much academic momentum was she losing?

Anne blamed Gavin's heart attack on years of working too hard and his stubborn insistence that "deep-fried" was a valid food group. But it was no coincidence that the man had collapsed during one of Vicki's multiple surgeries. The stress of his daughter's ordeal had nearly killed him.

"Jarrett." Anne's scolding tone was one he knew well from childhood. "I see you beating yourself up. You have to stop. If not for yourself, then for me."

"I'm fine," he lied. She was shouldering enough burden already without fretting over his well-being, too. "I was just processing the logistics of running the Twisted R while taking care of Vicki. I'll figure it out. You and Dad should definitely go."

"Thank you. Be sure to voice your support when he objects to the idea." She pursed her lips, considering. "We probably have a better shot at convincing him if you're *not* handling Vicki and the ranch by yourself. What if we found a part-time housekeeper who could act as her companion? Or, ideally, even someone with medical experience. My friend Pam's a retired nurse. I can ask her about home health care."

"Are we sure that's in the budget?" The mountain of medical bills was already high enough that Gavin had recently let go of their sole ranch hand after helping him find a job on another spread. Gavin insisted the Twisted R could function as a father-and-son operation if Jarrett was available to help full-time. No more rodeos for the foreseeable future.

Or ever. He hadn't competed since the night of Vicki's accident, and it was hard to imagine enjoying it again. Everything he'd loved—the adrenaline, the admiration of the spectators—seemed shallow in light of what his sister and dad had suffered.

"I'm not suggesting we hire a long-term employee," she said. "Just some help for a month or less. We have plenty of space. Maybe with Pam's help we can find someone temporarily willing to accept low pay in exchange for room and board. There could be someone young who needs the experience and a recommendation."

His mother made it sound almost reasonable, as if there were lots of people who would work practically for free and wanted to move in with a surly nineteen-year-old and a rodeo cowboy who'd taken early retirement. *What are the odds?*

Then again, they had to be due for some good luck.

"Okay," he agreed. "Call Pam and see what she says."

Meanwhile, he'd cross his fingers that his mom's friend knew someone who was truly desperate for a job.

"WHAT THE HELL do you mean I'm out of a job?" In her head, Sierra Bailey heard the familiar refrain of her mother's voice chiding her. Unladylike language was one of Muriel Bailey's pet peeves. *I just got fired. Screw "ladylike."*

Eileen Pearce, seated at the head of the conference table, sucked in a breath at Sierra's outburst. It was too bad Eileen and Muriel didn't live in the same city— the two women could get together for weekly coffee and commiserate about Sierra's behavior. "The board takes inappropriate relationships with patients very seriously, Ms. Bailey."

"There was no relationship!" Except, apparently, in Lloyd Carson's mind. Bodily contact between patient and physical therapist was a necessity, not an attempt at seduction. Sierra had never once thought of Lloyd in a sexual manner, but he'd apparently missed that memo. The man had unexpectedly kissed her during their last session. Which, in turn, led to his wife angrily demanding Sierra's head on a platter.

Taking a deep breath, Sierra battled her temper. "Patients become infatuated with medical professionals all the time. It's a form of misplaced gratitude and—"

"Yes, but in the year you've been with us, we've had multiple complaints about you. Granted, not of this nature, but your track record is flawed. Perhaps if you'd listened on previous occasions when I tried to impress upon you the importance of professional decorum..." Eileen paused with an expression of mock sympathy.

Comprehension dawned. This wasn't about Lloyd Carson and his romantic delusions. The board of directors had been looking for an excuse to get rid of Sierra. She felt foolish, not having seen the dismissal coming, but she truly believed she was good at her job.

Was she mouthy and abrasive? Occasionally.

All right, regularly. One might even argue, frequently. But sometimes PT patients needed a well-intentioned kick to the rear more than they needed to be coddled. *Lord knows I did.*

At twelve years old, Sierra had been a pampered rich girl whose parents treated her with a much different standard than her three rough-and-tumble brothers, as if she were fragile. Dr. Frederick Bailey and his wife, Muriel, had raised their sons with aspirations of global domination; they'd raised their daughter with the promise that she'd be a beautiful Houston debutante someday. No one had challenged her until the gruff physiotherapist who'd helped her after she'd been thrown from a horse.

He'd taught her to challenge herself, a lesson she still appreciated fifteen years later. The side effect was that she also tended to challenge authority, a habit the hospital's board of directors resented.

Given the barely concealed hostility in Eileen's icy blue gaze, it was a miracle Sierra had lasted this long. *You're partially to blame here, Bailey.* While she'd deny with every breath in her body that her conduct with Lloyd Carson had ever been flirtatious or unprofessional, Sierra could have been more of a team player. She could have made an effort to care about occupational politics.

As Eileen went over the legal details of the termination, Sierra's mind wandered to the future. Her savings account was skimpier than she'd like, but she was a trained specialist. She'd land on her feet. It was a point of pride that she'd been making her way for years, without asking her parents for money.

You'll find a new position. And when you do? Stay under the radar instead of racking up a file of grievances. In the interests of her career, Sierra could be detached and diplomatic.

Probably.

Chapter Two

"Darling, you're being needlessly stubborn," Muriel Bailey chastised through the phone. "Coming home for an extended visit would be a win for everyone. Since you aren't busy with work—"

"I'm busy looking for a job." Word had spread through the medical grapevine from Dallas to Houston that Sierra had been fired. Ever since Muriel had learned about it last week, she'd been relentlessly campaigning for Sierra to move back to Houston. *There's a better chance of my being elected president and moving to the White House.*

Her mother sighed. "But it's always difficult to get vacation time approved after starting a new position. What if they won't give you the days off for your brother's wedding?" According to Muriel, Kyle's December nuptials would be The Social Event of the Decade. "I need you here so you can help me with the millions of details! Then you'll start job-hunting again after the holidays. New year, new career."

Trapped under her parents' roof from September until January? Little spots appeared in front of Sierra's eyes, and she gripped the edge of the granite-topped kitchen island for support. "I'll be sure to mention that my brother is getting married during interviews and give prospective employers a heads-up." Assuming she got any more interviews.

By affronting the hospital's board of directors, she seemed to have damaged her options here in Dallas. Only two people had been willing to meet with her so far—a sleaze who'd ogled her breasts throughout the entire conversation and a sycophant who'd gushed about what an honor it was to meet the daughter of esteemed Chief of Neurosurgery Frederick Bailey. She didn't want to take a job that was offered because of who her father was, but if nothing better materialized...

"Sierra, are you even listening to me?"

"Um." Not for the past five minutes or so. "I may have missed that last part."

"Douglas Royce has been asking about you. He can't wait to see you at the wedding."

Oh, for pity's sake. Her mother couldn't possibly think there was still a chance Sierra might one day become Mrs. Douglas Royce? Opening the fridge, she searched for a bottle of wine. *Damn.* The downside of no paycheck was a serious lack of groceries. "We broke up years ago."

"Yet you haven't had a serious relationship since! Perhaps because, deep down, you—"

"Paul and I were plenty serious." Just not transcontinental serious. When Dr. Paul Meadows had left a couple of months ago to do medical work in Africa, they'd shared an affectionate goodbye. It was true she hadn't dated much between Douglas and Paul, but three years of grad school and twelve months of residency hadn't left much free time. "You're conveniently forgetting, I never loved Douglas half as much as you and Dad did. So you're not going to use him to lure me home."

"Parents shouldn't have to 'lure' their own flesh and blood. Where's your sense of familial duty?" Muriel huffed. "Who's going to help me with this mountain of wedding tasks?"

Sierra supposed it would be sheer lunacy to suggest the bride. Was poor Annabel getting *any* say in her big day? *I warned Kyle they should elope.* "Don't be afraid to delegate to the zillion-dollar-an-hour wedding coordinator, Mom. That's what Annabel's family is paying her for. I hate to cut this short, but I have a phone interview this evening." Could her lie have sounded less convincing?

"Really? With whom?"

"Um…" Sierra rubbed her temple. "Oh, I think that's my other line. Gotta go, love to Dad, 'bye!" She disconnected before her mother could respond, poured a glass of water and went to the living room, where her laptop sat on the couch. For a moment, she considered checking flights to Africa. Maybe she should follow Paul's example—go help people in another part of the world and put an ocean between her and her parents.

Instead, she checked email to see if her job search had netted any new responses, then fired off a quick note to Kyle.

Subject: Our Mother Is Off The Rails
Annabel must REALLY love you to put up with Mom. Hope you know what a lucky guy you are. See you in December—and not a single day sooner! S.

Her brother never replied to any of her messages. No doubt he was too busy plotting corporate take-overs.

She started to close her email, but her gaze lingered on a name in her inbox. Daniel Baron. He'd written to her two days ago, but she still hadn't decided whether to act on the information he'd passed along.

Daniel was a former bull rider and past patient. She'd reached out to him last week when it became clear she needed more references. Not only had Daniel been happy to hear from her and more than willing to endorse her, he'd learned of an unusual job posting through a friend of a friend. He'd told her about a family in Cupid's Bow, Texas. She'd almost rolled her eyes at the town name, but she supposed it was no quirkier than Gun Barrel City, Texas. Or Ding Dong, Texas.

According to Daniel, the teenage daughter of the family had been in an accident, and the Rosses were looking for someone to live on the ranch and work with the kid for about a month. A ranch…where there were horses. She shuddered.

I am not a small-town person. But she prided herself on being tough when she needed to be, and it wouldn't be a long-term situation. With a guaranteed roof over her head, she would have time to investigate other opportunities. Three and a half weeks could make the difference between finding a position where she truly fit and simply accepting a paycheck so she could continue indulging in luxuries like food and water.

After she'd first read Daniel's email, she'd looked up Cupid's Bow online. It was tiny. Her parents' country club probably had a higher population—ironic, since the club worked at actively excluding people. Sierra doubted there were any symphony performances or science museums in Cupid's Bow. But worse than a potential dearth of culture or even the presence of horses was the possibility of nosy neighbors. Weren't people in close-knit communities subject to scrutiny and gossip? Given her parents' wealth and high social standing, Sierra had spent her teen years feeling conspicuously visible. People who'd never even met her had opinions about who she was and who they thought she should be. She detested feeling as if she had to answer anyone.

All right then, don't call the Rosses. Stay here and get a job waitressing. With your gracious nature, you're sure to make enough tips to pay off those student loans.

Lord. No wonder she couldn't get a job—she even gave herself attitude.

Decision made, she pulled her phone from her pocket before she could change her mind. As she dialed, she reminded herself there was no guarantee the Rosses would hire her. If they did, she'd survive roughing it in Cupid's Bow one day at a time. How many times had she lectured patients on the necessity of breaking down tasks into less intimidating chunks?

"Quit looking at it as months of PT," she'd tell them. *"Just get through each set of exercises, one day at a time. This first set's only ten minutes. It may be uncomfortable, but you can handle ten measly minutes. Don't wuss out on me now..."*

She cajoled, encouraged and berated people into cooperating. The least she could do was take her own advice.

The phone rang, and she inhaled deeply. After a

couple more rings, she began mentally rehearsing the message she would leave on the voice mail. But then a man answered.

"Hello?" The irritation in his deep voice made the word less a greeting and more a challenge.

She hesitated, but for only half a second. Tentativeness wasn't in her nature. "May I speak with Jarrett Ross?"

"You got him. But if you're selling something—"

"Only my professional services." Someone should tell Mr. Ross that anyone who placed a Help Wanted ad should curb his hostility; it made people not want to help. "My name is Sierra Bailey. I'm a physical therapist, and Daniel Baron, one of my former clients, gave me this number. He mentioned your family is looking for someone with PT experience."

"Oh! Yes. God, yes. Sorry, you just caught me at a bad time. Of course, that describes all of the time lately, but— Sorry," he repeated. "I wasn't expecting applicants to call me. Most of them have been phoning my mother."

"Ah. You're not the girl's father?" Daniel had given her a name and a number. He hadn't outlined the family tree.

"Definitely not. I'm Vicki's older brother. But I might as well talk to you. After all, you and I would be the ones living together while my parents are away."

Living together. The words gave her an odd jolt. Although Paul had spent enough nights at her place to warrant his own dresser drawer and a sliver of counter space in the bathroom, she'd never technically lived with a man. *You wouldn't be living with this one, either.* Not in any personal way.

"My parents' trip is why we're seeking the extra

help with Vicki," he continued. "Not only could she benefit from physical therapy here at the house, we could use someone to keep her company while I'm working the ranch. If she needs something, I'm not readily accessible on the back forty. What was your name again?"

"Sierra. Sierra Bailey."

"And Daniel Baron gave you my number? He's a good guy. I used to compete against him and his brothers all the time."

"Ah. So you're a rodeo rider." She hadn't meant to sound judgmental. It just wasn't a lifestyle she could wrap her head around. She worked with so many people who were injured through no fault of their own that it was hard to understand anyone deliberately pursuing such a potentially dangerous career.

"I was," he said tightly, "but not anymore. I'm committed to the ranch. And to Vicki's recovery."

The patient. Here was comfortable ground. In her other interviews, she'd had to talk about herself, which made her prickly. It was easier to sound competent and professional while discussing the person she'd be treating.

She asked about the girl's age—nineteen was older than she'd expected—and injuries. There was a pause before Jarrett began describing them. When he started talking again, the words came in an uncomfortable rush, as if he wanted to get through the list as quickly as possible. His younger sister was healing from several injuries, including a broken wrist, but the major issue was that her pelvis had been crushed in the accident.

Sierra winced. It was the kind of pity she'd never

show in front of a patient because pity made a person feel weak. But the young woman had a rough time ahead of her.

"You obviously know your field well," Jarrett said after they'd spent a few minutes discussing medical specifics. Yet he sounded more grim than impressed. Wasn't her expertise a *good* thing? "To tell you the truth, Ms. Bailey, you may be overqualified. We were thinking more in terms of a semiretired therapist or a home health care assistant who might not mind some light housekeeping and making sure Vicki gets dinner if I'm working past sundown. I don't know if Daniel mentioned salary, but—"

"He did." Calling that sum a salary was a generous overstatement. "It's below what I would normally consider, but honestly, I'm taking some time off to decide between several future options." Yeah, like whether to waitress at a steak house or bartend at a West End nightclub. "This gives me time to carefully evaluate my choices." *Well done, Bailey.* She'd managed to make herself sound methodical, not desperate.

"So you're all right with our terms?"

"Well, I won't argue if you decide after a week that I deserve a raise, but what you're offering is at least worth my driving to Cupid's Bow for a face-to-face meeting."

"That's fantastic." It was the happiest he'd sounded during their entire conversation, and it highlighted how dour his mood had been—from his tense tone when he'd answered to his obvious discomfort discussing his sister's accident to his doubt Sierra would deem the job worth it. Jarrett Ross clearly wasn't the president of the Cupid's Bow Optimists Club. "I just wish my parents hadn't already booked their flight. They're leaving in two days, so unless you can be here tomorrow, they won't be available to sit in on the interview."

"Sorry, tomorrow's full." Since she hadn't known where and when she'd be working again, she'd scheduled a number of personal appointments, taking advantage of the time left before her health and dental insurance ran out. "I can manage the next day, though."

They agreed on a time, and he asked for her email address so he could send her directions. "GPS or internet maps will get you most of the way, but we're a bit off the beaten path."

Which didn't bolster her enthusiasm for making a temporary home in Cupid's Bow.

Then again, if the town could evade the reach of an orbiting satellite system, she should easily be outside the meddling reach of Muriel Bailey. Ever since Sierra's last relationship ended, her mother, undaunted by living three and a half hours away, had tried arranging meetings between Sierra and Dallas's most eligible bachelors. The good news about a town the size of Cupid's Bow was that there couldn't be many men who met her mother's exacting standards.

So when she ended her call with Jarrett by saying "I look forward to meeting you," she very nearly meant it.

Chapter Three

"Knock, knock," Jarrett said tentatively, unsure of his welcome as he stood in the doorway of his sister's room. His voice seemed to echo unnaturally. The house had been damned quiet in the hours since their parents had left at the crack of dawn. According to his mother, Vicki had barely said a word when they came into her room to exchange goodbyes. Did she feel like the Rosses were abandoning her?

His mother was excited that Jarrett was interviewing another candidate this afternoon. Until Sierra had called, the family had decided to offer the position to local retired nurse Lucy Aldridge, a grandmother of five. Lucy was kind, if a bit absentminded, but she was also more than three times Vicki's age. Anne Ross had worried Vicki wouldn't relate to her. Jarrett didn't know specifically how old Sierra Bailey was, but judging from the credentials she'd emailed, she'd been out of med school for only a couple of years. And she certainly hadn't sounded like a woman approaching seventy. When they'd spoken, Sierra had sounded… *Feisty* was the word that sprang to mind.

"Did you need something?" Vicki asked, her voice empty of inflection. Her wheelchair was pulled up to her desk, and he couldn't tell if she was looking at her laptop or simply staring out the window. This used to be a guest suite, but since it was on the first floor, they'd relocated Vicki after the accident. All the essentials were here, but she'd said not to bother with miscellaneous belongings, like the posters that hung on her walls upstairs. Or the gleaming softball trophies that sent blades of guilt through him whenever he saw them.

Her blond hair hung crookedly in a limp ponytail. She was able to shower by herself in the remodeled bathroom, but she only bothered to brush her hair when her mother said something about it. And the last time she'd applied makeup was when her boyfriend, Aaron, had visited weeks ago.

"I just wanted to remind you that Sierra should be here in an hour or so." When Vicki didn't respond, he prompted, "Sierra Bailey, the potential therapist. I thought you might like to meet her."

She hadn't sat in on any of the interviews, dismissing it as unnecessary. All of the candidates had been local, which meant she'd met them all at least in passing. Anne hadn't pushed the issue, since she'd already had her hands full convincing Gavin to leave the ranch. Jarrett was surprised by his sister's apathy. Vicki had always been opinionated. Surely she wanted to have a say in who was chosen to be her companion?

"I'll pass," she said. "I was about to take a nap. I'm exhausted."

From all the energy it took to stare out the window? *Don't be an ass. You don't know anything about the effort it takes her to perform daily tasks you take for granted.* Besides, fatigue wasn't always physical.

He attempted a compromise. "If she seems like a good fit for the job, do you want me to wake you up before she leaves? Then you could—"

"No." She shot a glance over her shoulder. It was jarring how her dark eyes flashed with so much emotion while her clipped words held none at all. "Makes no difference to me who pushes my wheelchair."

Nobody pushed the chair. They'd rented an electric one to make her as self-sufficient as possible. "Vicki—"

"I don't care who you hire, just make it clear she's not my babysitter. And anytime Aaron visits, we want our privacy."

He clenched his jaw, conflicted about his little sister's "alone time" with her boyfriend. *Hypocrite. Like you were celibate at nineteen?* Hell no. He'd always been ready and willing to hit the sheets with a pretty lady—a character trait he deeply regretted. If he'd had any self-discipline, Vicki wouldn't be in the wheelchair. Or in this room. She'd be at college with Aaron and her friends.

"Close the door on your way out," she said woodenly.

"Okay." As conversations went, he couldn't call this one a rousing success. On the other hand, it was the most sentences she'd spoken to him at one time all month. Maybe his mother was right about his parents' trip forcing Vicki to deal with him. Jarrett just wished his sister would let loose and scream at him. Call him an irresponsible ass. Maybe even hurl something at him with that pitcher's arm of hers. She'd broken her left wrist, but her right was undamaged.

He went to the kitchen, where he pulled a casserole from the freezer for its two hours in the oven and brewed iced tea for his expected guest. He'd briefly spoken to Daniel Baron this week about Sierra. The man sang her praises. Daniel had worked with her after the bull-riding injury that made him quit rodeo for good, not that he sounded disappointed about his new lifestyle. He was happily married in San Antonio with twin toddlers. If Sierra was under fifty and even half as promising as Daniel made her sound, she had a job.

While he waited for Sierra to arrive, Jarrett caught up on emails and the paperwork that accumulated while he spent most of his time outside. In addition to taking care of the cattle and preparing to plant the winter crops, he generated income by offering riding lessons and equine therapy. He was happier doing physical work than crunching numbers, but it was on his shoulders to make sure nothing fell through the cracks while his father recuperated.

He'd just finished entering some figures in the banking spreadsheet when the doorbell rang. If either the golden retriever or shepherd-Lab mix had been close to the house, he would have heard barking long before the visitor reached the front porch, but in pretty weather, the dogs enjoyed the wide-open spaces of ranch life.

In case his sister had been genuine about needing sleep, he hurried to the door to make sure Sierra didn't ring the bell a second time. Mentally crossing his fingers that the woman on the other side was everything Daniel said, he swung the door open.

He felt his features freeze midsmile. Shock made it momentarily difficult to form words, even one as basic as *hello*. He'd been hoping for younger than fifty, but the stunning redhead appeared to be in her twenties. And, although his mama would smack him upside the head for the stereotype, she looked more like a lingerie model than a med school graduate.

Well, technically, she was probably too short to be a model, but that body... "Sierra Bailey?" he asked, half hoping she wasn't.

She nodded. "Jarrett Ross?"

"One and the same." As he ushered her inside, he tried to recover his composure. The view from behind wasn't helping. Her slim-fitting suit skirt fell just below her knees, modestly professional, but the material lovingly cupped the flare of her hips and shapely butt.

Squeezing his eyes shut, he spared a dark thought for Daniel Baron. His friend should have warned Jarrett what to expect. Daniel was so head over heels in love with his wife, Nicole, that other women probably paled in comparison, but the man wasn't blind.

The irony would have been laughable if Jarrett's sense of humor weren't dormant. He hadn't had sex in months. He'd ignored flirty texts and used the isolation of the ranch to avoid temptation, but that hadn't been penance enough. Karma had sent him a gorgeous woman whose green eyes flashed intelligence and whose curves would make a centerfold envious. His past self would have found sleeping down the hall from her a tantalizing prospect.

Hell, the old Jarrett would already be working to seduce her. But he was a recovering ladies' man and, potentially, her employer. *You will not so much as look at Sierra Bailey.*

Too late.

IT WAS TOO soon to tell whether this interview would be an improvement over her others, but, so far, it was certainly *weirder*. Sierra had entered the house ready to apologize for being late. She'd got lost twice, not that she'd been able to call Jarrett Ross and tell him because she'd apparently been driving through a cellular dead zone. She'd finally happened across a tiny gas station where a friendly guy with elaborate tattoos gave her directions to the Twisted R.

She knew it was bad form to show up tardy to an interview, but before she'd had a chance to explain, Jarrett had suddenly declared, "Tea!" the way a scientist might shout "Eureka!" Then he'd pointed her into a wood-paneled study and bolted in the opposite direction. Presumably, to fetch tea.

Her first impression of the rancher was that he was tall—although, from her perspective, lots of people were. More specifically, he was hot. His dark hair, threaded with a few sun-streaked threads of gold, contrasted dramatically with pale silvery eyes. He had a chiseled jaw and defined cheekbones.

And abs worthy of inspiring legend.

That highly unprofessional observation struck as she caught sight of a framed picture among the dozen or so that hung on the far wall behind a massive desk. In the photo, a shirtless Jarrett stood on the shore of a river, displaying a fish he'd caught. She was already moving in for a closer look before she realized what she was doing, as if mindlessly drawn in by a tractor beam. *Tractor abs.* Plus, sculpted shoulders and arms that—

Bailey! What the hell happened to being professional?

Right.

It was ironic that she'd been fired over Lloyd Carson, given that she'd never entertained a single thought about him half as improper as what she'd just been feeling for Jarrett Ross. *Get your act together.* She moved on from the shirtless picture to the other shots decorating the wall. Several had been taken at rodeos, and while she'd never understand bronc-riding as a career choice, she had to marvel at the raw grace displayed in one action shot. Repressing the memory of her own horrific fall from a horse, she wondered how Jarrett managed to stay in the saddle. For that matter, how was the black cowboy hat staying on his head?

Next to that photo was a snapshot taken right here on the house's front porch. Jarrett's arm was casually draped around a blonde girl's shoulders. Sierra was willing to bet money that the young woman was his sister, Vicki. Their coloring was reversed—the girl had light hair and brown eyes—but the similarity of their features was unmistakable. As was the affection between them.

Sierra glanced from Vicki's face to Jarrett's. His expression was so self-assured. He was grinning as though he didn't have a care in the world, and his eyes sparkled with mischief and confidence—a far cry from the somber man who'd opened the door to her.

She supposed no one chose to display family photos where the subject was scowling or looked troubled, but his image was the same in every picture—the self-satisfied lord of all he surveyed. Was it Vicki's accident that had changed him? Sierra knew a lot of siblings were closer than she was to her own brothers. Jarrett had been notably tense while detailing his sister's injuries over the phone, as if he felt her pain.

Vicki may be the one in the wheelchair, but apparently she wasn't the only one who needed to heal.

Chapter Four

Sierra shifted her position in the leather chair and sipped her sweet tea, waiting for Jarrett to say something. They'd reached the end of his list of questions, and she assumed he was mulling over her responses. He hadn't said anything in several seconds. He'd been terse throughout the conversation, lending credence to the strong, silent cowboy image, but, on the bright side, he hadn't mentioned her family connections or leered at her. He'd barely looked at her at all, either focusing on the pad of paper where he was jotting notes or staring at some point just over her shoulder.

The interview had reached its logical conclusion. All that was left was for her to talk to the patient and assess for herself the work that needed to be done. Jarrett had handed her a folder of medical records after joining her in the study with two glasses of iced tea, but X-rays told only part of the story.

Sierra set her glass on the desk and cleared her throat. "When can I meet Vicki?"

His head jerked up, his eyes almost meeting hers before he resumed that unfocused gaze into the beyond. "Oh, uh, that won't be necessary. She's sleeping now and authorized me to make the decision on her behalf. And I'm happy to say, the job is yours. If you want it."

Fantastic. She was employed again—by a laconic cowboy who lived at the butt-end of nowhere and kept staring eerily into space as if he were about to have a psychic vision. "Thank you for the offer. I'll be able to give you my answer after I meet your sister."

He frowned. "I told you, she's sleeping."

She rose from her chair, eager to escape the awkward confines of the study. "So we'll need to wake her up." Every patient case she'd ever worked had started with an evaluation. And this wasn't just any case—she'd be living with these people! No way was she packing her bags and relocating before meeting both of her new roommates.

Jarrett's gaze locked with hers, and the sudden connection was like an electric current that ran all the way down to her toes. The masculine energy in his rigid body language caused a wholly inappropriate tingly sensation. She could almost understand how a stupid cliché like "you're beautiful when you're angry" had originated.

"Vicki expressly asked not to be disturbed," he said, his sharp tone matching the metallic glint in his eyes.

Sierra lifted her chin, determined to make him see reason. "Is she ill?" If the girl was sick, then Sierra would come back another day to meet her—especially if Vicki was contagious. Otherwise...

"You mean like with a cold or something? No. But, as a professional, you must know that people recuperating from such serious injuries need plenty of bed rest and—"

"It's been a couple of months since her accident. Too much bed rest leads to atrophy. I've been here over an hour," she said with a glance at her watch. "That's adequate for a nap. Sleeping the day away can also be a sign of depression. Part of my job will be keeping Vicki engaged, whether she likes it or not."

"You mean bullying her?" he asked. The way he shot to his feet, as if preparing to physically protect his sister, might have been endearing under other circumstances.

"I wouldn't say 'bullying.'" *She* might not put it that way...but a few of her patients had. Bully. Drill sergeant. Hard-ass. Daniel Baron, sweating through a session with his handsome features contorted into a grimace, had once called her a demon tyrant with no soul. But she was pretty sure he'd meant it as a compliment.

"Look, I'm good at what I do," she asserted. "If you want me to take this job, you have to trust me."

Nice going, Bailey. Three minutes after he offers you the position and you're already giving ultimatums. What happened to demure and diplomatic and all that other crap?

He clenched his jaw, and she wondered uneasily if he would throw her out. Then he shoved a hand through his hair, the anger in his expression fading. "She's my responsibility." It didn't sound like a protest, more like...a plea.

Her heart twisted at the jagged vulnerability in his voice. She added "lack of professional detachment" to her list of today's sins.

Jarrett sighed, rounding the desk toward her. "Come on. Let's get this over with."

LAST SPRING, JARRETT had subdued a towering drunk intent on a bar fight until Sheriff Trent and Deputy Thomas could get there. During the summer, he'd calmly faced an angry bull and the occasional venomous copperhead. But women? They were scary.

Caught between Vicki's inevitable displeasure and Sierra's implacable resolve, he held his breath and knocked on the closed bedroom door. Normally, he did just fine with ladies, but now he was trapped in a house with two females he couldn't charm. His sister was immune, and flirting with an employee was unethical.

A rebellious part of his brain that didn't care about ethics wondered, if he *were* free to flirt with Sierra, how would she respond?

She was tough, with an unyielding force of will, hardly a woman who batted her lashes and giggled when a guy looked in her direction. Yet there'd been a sizzling moment in the study when their eyes met and— He broke off the thought. What had happened to not allowing himself to lust after the therapist?

Annoyed at his lack of discipline, he banged his fist against the door a bit harder this time. Still no response.

"She's not answering." From behind him, Sierra stated the obvious. Her palpable impatience was a vibration in the air. He could just imagine the nuclear confrontation when her hardheaded personality clashed with his sister's. Was it a mistake to hire the redhead instead of sweet-natured Lucy Aldridge, who would affectionately fuss over Vicki as if she were an honorary grandchild?

"We should go in," she urged.

Nearly a month of this woman bossing him around? Jarrett ground his teeth. "I'm not in the habit of invading her privacy."

Sierra's hand curved over his shoulder, surprising him, and when he turned to meet her gaze, he saw genuine concern. "You'd be checking to make sure she's okay. The way you've described her state of mind…"

He turned the knob and shoved the door open a few inches. "Vicki?"

She was lying on her back with her eyes closed, but her features were creased with aggravation. "I'm *trying* to sleep. Go away."

Sierra squeezed past him into the room. "Since you're awake, I was hoping we could talk."

At the unfamiliar voice, Vicki opened her eyes. "Now's not a good time." She glared past the redhead at her brother. "I'd appreciate you not letting strangers into my room."

"I—"

"Not a stranger for long," Sierra interrupted cheerfully. "I'm your new physical therapist. Sierra Bailey. Pleased to meet you."

Jarrett wasn't sure when she'd officially accepted the job, but he didn't undermine her authority by asking the question out loud.

Sierra took a step closer to the bed, nodding toward the brace that covered most of Vicki's forearm. "Are you regularly seeing a therapist about your wrist?"

Vicki grunted a sound that was more or less agreement.

"How much have you been working at home?" Sierra asked, switching to a question that required a more specific answer.

"When I can. It hurts."

"The more you build your strength—within medically approved parameters, of course—the faster you'll heal. What exercises have you been doing?"

"You're the one who needs this job," Vicki snapped. "Shouldn't *I* be doing the interrogating?"

Folding his arms across his chest, Jarrett waited to see how Sierra dealt with his sister's uncooperative attitude. He knew from their exchange back in his dad's study that the redhead had a temper.

Yet Sierra's tone was only one of mild reproach when she said, "I didn't realize you had any questions for me. According to your brother, you willingly forfeited any say in the decision-making process." She paused. "But if there's something you'd like to ask, fire away."

"Have you even been a therapist long enough to know what you're doing?" Vicki raked her over with an expression that made it clear she wasn't impressed with what she saw. "You barely look old enough to buy beer."

Despite the younger woman's sneering, Sierra smiled broadly. "Twenty-seven in November. But if you keep up the flattery, I might make it the whole time I'm here without trying to smother you."

Jarrett bit the inside of his cheek to keep from laughing. Technically speaking, it was poor bedside manner to threaten one's patients. But Vicki's outraged expression was downright encouraging. It reminded him of fights they'd had in years past, when she'd been whole and spirited. He'd take her anger any day of the week over the hollow-eyed stare she'd developed.

Although he'd wanted to gauge how the two females interacted without his interference, now he spoke up on Sierra's behalf, defending his hiring decision. "Ms.

Bailey's well qualified for her job—educated and experienced. According to Daniel Baron, she's one of the best in the state of Texas."

Sierra glanced back, looking surprised by the endorsement. The smile she flashed him decimated his vow not to notice how attractive she was.

"Thank you. But it's silly to call me Ms. Bailey. We should be on a first-name basis since we'll be living together. Who knows—by this time next month, we'll probably all have nicknames for each other."

"I have a few ideas," Vicki muttered.

"So do I. As for my qualifications, I graduated college early and finished my med school program at the top of the class. Before that, I logged hundreds of volunteer hours in clinics and my high school athletic department, learning from the trainers. I've been learning everything I can about physical therapy since a PT helped me after I fractured my spine. You're not the only one held together with screws and plates," she added softly.

Jarrett was caught off guard by this revelation. During their conversations on the phone and in the study, she'd never volunteered why she'd chosen the field. He hadn't thought to ask. With the knowledge that they'd faced similar obstacles, maybe Vicki would—

"We're not gonna be besties just because we've both had surgery," his sister said.

"Definitely not," Sierra agreed. "I don't do 'bonding.'"

Oddly, the disdainful words seemed to mollify his sister.

Vicki was quiet for a long moment. "You've only asked me about my wrist. Why not the big thing?"

"You mean the fact that you're in a wheelchair? Don't let that loom large in your mind as The Big Thing. In principle, the broken pelvis is just like the broken wrist. Both are physical challenges you can overcome with time to heal and lots of hard work. The question is, are you willing to do the work?"

When Vicki slowly nodded, something like hope shining in her dark eyes, Jarrett knew he owed Daniel Baron a debt of gratitude. Sierra Bailey was definitely the right woman for the job.

DINNER THAT NIGHT was quiet, and as he washed off the plates, Jarrett found himself anxiously awaiting Sierra's return in two days. He'd always loved the spacious ranch house, but with just him and his sullen sister, the empty space around them magnified the silence. That wouldn't be the case when Sierra moved in. Despite being a petite woman, she somehow filled an entire room with her energy.

Jarrett had invited her to stay for supper after her conversation with Vicki, but she'd insisted she needed to get going as soon as possible.

"The sun's setting earlier every day," she'd pointed out, "and I need to get at least somewhere *close* to civilization before it's completely dark. If I never return, it's because I got lost on one of your meandering, quaintly unmarked roads. Seriously, is there like a town ordinance against signs?"

In the short time she'd been at the ranch, she'd made several comments suggesting Cupid's Bow was not her ideal location. Thank God she'd agreed to take the position anyway. He glanced to where Vicki sat at the table, trying to touch her thumb to her finger. It was one of the exercises Sierra had insisted Vicki do.

"You follow this regimen exactly until I get back," Sierra had said, handing over a sheet of paper. "Or incur my wrath."

Vicki had rolled her eyes. "You really scare me, shorty."

Was it wishful thinking on Jarrett's part or had there *almost* been a smile in her voice? Even though parts of his sister's encounter with Sierra had been contentious, it was still the most animated he'd seen her in weeks—not counting the infrequent times her doofus boyfriend bothered to phone.

Jarrett had no real reason to dislike Aaron, but seeing how much those short conversations meant to his sister, he resented that the guy couldn't make time in his busy college schedule to call more often. *Or maybe Aaron's inattention makes you feel guilty because you know damn well there are women who probably expected a call from you that never came.*

He balled up the dish towel and threw it on the counter. "You ready to try that rice thing?" Sierra had left instructions for Jarrett to fill a bucket with dry rice and for Vicki to place her hand inside and try to rotate it. The rice would provide resistance.

The physical therapist had arched an eyebrow at Vicki. "Resistance is right up your alley, yeah?"

Jarrett went into the walk-in pantry for a bag of rice without waiting for his sister's answer—these days, he couldn't always count on her to give him one. When he joined her at the table, she was still doing the first set of exercises, wincing in visible pain. He desperately wanted to say something helpful, but what? The closest he could come to empathizing with what she was going through were the many bruises and sore muscles that came with riding rodeo. He'd voluntarily endured those because he liked to win. There was nothing voluntary about her suffering.

As she slid her left hand into the bucket, he tried to sound encouraging. "Sierra is highly recommended. Follow her advice, and I'm sure all of this will get easier." Eventually.

Beads of sweat dotted Vicki's forehead as she attempted to turn her wrist. "She's pretty, too. Like, obnoxiously pretty." She pinned him with her gaze. "Don't you think so?"

The question felt like a trap. Saying he hadn't noticed Sierra's appearance would be a ridiculous lie and an insult to his sister's intelligence. But survival instincts warned that admitting Sierra was beautiful would only increase the household tension. "I'm not sure what 'obnoxiously pretty' means."

"Well, she's way more fun for a guy to look at than old Lucy Aldridge."

The realization of what she was suggesting bit into him like barbwire through the skin. Shame bubbled to the surface instead of blood. His sister truly believed he was so selfish that he would hire the woman in charge of her well-being based on sex appeal? *Of course she does.* He had a track record of putting pleasure before loved ones or responsibility.

He clenched his hands into fists, and the reflexive action only heightened his guilt. He could move all ten of his fingers with no effort at all, while Vicki had gone pale in her wheelchair from trying to stir around grains of rice.

"Vic, I would have hired a wart-covered, hunch-backed troll if I thought she could get you better faster. Maybe some guys would find Sierra Bailey 'fun to look at,' but I won't be looking at her. I'll be working the ranch and staying out of her way so she can focus on you. Your recovery is all that matters to me."

She cast him a brief, skeptical glance before ducking her gaze without comment. The little sister who'd once idolized him no longer trusted him.

Why should she? He'd given her reason to doubt. *I know I let you down, Vic, but I swear it won't happen again.*

Chapter Five

Even though she'd packed up her car with luggage and turned off all her utilities, accepting the job with the Rosses didn't feel real until Sierra drove past the Welcome to Cupid's Bow sign on Saturday. *Sure, the town welcomes you—then they hide all the other road signs so you can never find your way back out.* Cupid's Bow, Texas. Come for the home cooking, stay for…ever.

On the phone last night, Muriel had asked, "Are you sure about this, darling? Living in some backwater town for a month when you could be at home with your loving family?"

If Sierra hadn't already been convinced that she should take the job, that would have done the trick.

Now, alone in the car, she reiterated what she'd said to her mother. "This is where I need to be right now." So why the nervous butterflies in her stomach? Anxiety that Vicki Ross would be a difficult patient?

No way. I am Sierra Bailey, and I eat difficulty for breakfast. I pour it into my coffee to give it that extra kick.

And yet…tummy flutters. She refused to even consider that they might be a reaction to seeing Jarrett Ross again. Sure, the rancher was good-looking, but she'd spent many hands-on hours working with hot athletes. She was *not* jittery about moving in with a tall, gray-eyed cowboy. The more likely explanation for her apprehensive stomach was that breakfast hadn't agreed with her.

There was a grocery store up ahead. She could stop for antacids and other essentials she'd want to have on hand for the next few weeks. Plus, Jarrett had mentioned that grocery shopping and meal preparation would be part of her job. Might as well investigate the supermarket's selection and get her bearings.

Fifteen minutes later, she'd discovered that the local produce prices were fantastic and that she didn't own enough denim to fit in around Cupid's Bow. The two pairs of jeans she did own were in a suitcase in her car; she felt conspicuous in her circle skirt, swirled with autumn colors, and green chenille V-neck sweater. The only people she'd seen who weren't wearing jeans either wore denim shorts or overalls.

Rounding an endcap, she pushed the cart into the pharmaceutical section, gratified to spot a blonde woman, her hair pulled back in a loose French braid, wearing a sundress not made of denim. The bright geometric print and pattern of straps holding the bodice in place made the outfit fashionable without looking ostentatious.

"Love your dress," she said impulsively.

Turning from the shelf of vitamins she'd been contemplating, the woman flashed her a bright smile. "Thank you. All that jazz."

"I… Pardon?"

"The boutique just off of town square," the woman clarified. "All That Jazz. Run by Jasmine Tucker?"

She grinned at Sierra's blank expression. "You must not be from around here."

At that moment, a teenage boy with a little girl in tow barreled toward them. They weren't running, exactly, just moving at the uninhibited speed of childhood. "Mom! They didn't have the brand you normally get," the boy announced, skidding to a stop by his mother's cart. "Will one of these work?" He held up two different boxes of cake mix.

Before the woman could answer, the little girl in the unicorn T-shirt tossed a box of crayons into the cart. "I need these."

"Doubtful," the boy scoffed. "You own more crayons than anyone else in North America, Aly."

"These are *scented*. I don't have scented." At Sierra's chuckle, the girl looked up, registering her presence for the first time. "Hey, we don't know you!"

Sierra shook her head. "Nope. Today's my very first day in town."

"Welcome to Cupid's Bow," the blonde said. "I'm Kate Sullivan. This is my son, Luke, and my future stepdaughter Alyssa."

"She's marrying my daddy!" From the huge smile on Alyssa's face, she was obviously excited about the upcoming nuptials. "Me and my sister get to be flower girls, and we're gonna wear poofy dresses that—"

"How about you go with Luke and return the cake mix we don't need?" Kate interrupted, taking one of the boxes from her son's hand. "And don't run, okay?"

"Okay," the kids chorused without looking back at her.

"And they're off," Kate said with an affectionate sigh. "I came to the vitamin section to get more gummies for the girls, but, honestly, maybe I should be looking for a supplement for *me* so I can keep up with all of them. Let's try this again, with fewer interruptions. I'm Kate Sullivan." She extended a hand. "Nice to meet you."

"Sierra Bailey," she said as they shook hands.

"I'm so delighted you're moving here." Kate grinned. "With you around, people will have to stop referring to me as 'the new woman in Cupid's Bow.' It's been months!"

"Happy to help," Sierra said, "but I'm not moving here, exactly, just working for a few weeks at the Twisted R." Assuming she could successfully locate the ranch again.

"Oh!" A female voice from the other side of the shelf cut into their conversation and an elderly lady peeked over the top, only her tightly rolled white curls and gold spectacles visible. "Are you working with that poor Victoria Ross? Such a tragedy what happened to her. Hello, Kate, dear."

"Hello, Miss Alma. This is Sierra Bailey."

"I heard. My new hearing aids are a miracle. I hope you enjoy your stay here in Cupid's Bow, Sierra. You tell poor Vicki that the whole town's pulling for her." She clucked her tongue. "Absolute tragedy." A minute later, she pushed her cart away and disappeared down the bread aisle.

Kate smiled after her. "Not everyone is as active an eavesdropper as Miss Alma—she's almost ninety and says living here almost a century gives her a vested interest in local events—but this is a small town. We all heard about Vicki's accident. The Ross family hasn't been the same since."

"I haven't met her parents." She only knew they were traveling for "health reasons." "Just Vicki and her older brother."

"Jarrett. A real charmer, that one."

"He's…attractive," Sierra said neutrally. "But charming? For the first hour of my interview, he read questions verbatim off a legal pad and barely said anything else. I can count on one hand the number of times he even looked up at me."

The corners of Kate's mouth turned down, and sympathy filled her amber eyes. "After his dad's heart attack, I took some meals to the family. Jarrett was so shell-shocked, not himself at all. I haven't seen him recently, but I was hoping that with his father and Vicki both doing better… Well. I suppose we all cope in our own time, don't we?"

Sierra nodded. She'd witnessed patients and their families handle crisis in dozens of ways. Sometimes, catastrophes brought people together; other times it drove a wedge between them. There were patients who spiraled into a dark place and needed help finding their way back; others rebounded with astonishing resiliency.

Kate gave a small shake of her head, as if brushing away her moment of melancholy. "I live near the Twisted R—at least, I do until my wedding. My fiancé, Cole, and I are having a house built that won't be ready for months. Meanwhile, Luke and I are staying on my grandmother's farm, which is out the same direction as the Ross place. If you ever need anything, we're much closer than town. I'll give you my number. Maybe we can get together if you have an afternoon off."

"Thank you." Given Vicki Ross's surly attitude, Sierra might need to occasionally escape the ranch to keep her sanity intact. "I'd love to visit that boutique you were telling me about."

They had just finished exchanging cell-phone numbers when the two kids returned.

"Sorry we took so long," Luke said, jamming his hands in the pockets of his jeans. "I—"

"He was talking to a *girrrlll*," Aly reported, making the last word three syllables.

He shot her a sidelong glare. "I ran into a classmate—"

"A girl classmate!"

"—who had questions about Friday's math assignment."

"No problem," Kate said. "Sierra and I were busy chatting, too. But I guess we should dash if I'm going to get these groceries to Cole's house for lunch. He and Mandy are probably starving. Call me soon, Sierra!"

"Will do."

As she finished her own grocery shopping, Sierra felt a little smug. She'd been told more than once that she didn't play well with others and that some people mistook her independent nature for aloofness. Yet she hadn't been in town an hour, and already she'd made her first friend.

Maybe Cupid's Bow wouldn't be so bad after all.

JUST WHEN SIERRA was starting to think she'd driven too far, she spotted the intersection where she needed to turn for the Twisted R. On her first trip out to the ranch, she'd been irritable because she was late for her interview. This time around, she could appreciate the scenery more.

The wide-open space was both tranquil and somehow humbling. Picturesque pastures dotted with clusters of Queen Anne's lace and mesquite trees framed the road, and she'd never seen a clearer blue sky than the one overhead. A deer lifted its head from the plants it was lazily munching to watch her pass, and she half expected that if she glanced in her rearview mirror she'd find animated woodland creatures singing some kind of welcome song behind her car.

It was all very bucolic. But she still couldn't imagine living in a place where the closest store was half an hour away. *The land that delivery food forgot.*

She turned left onto a winding road barely wide enough for two vehicles to pass each other and saw the sprawling white house atop the hill ahead. She liked the Rosses' place—it wasn't as linear and pristine as her parents' three-story mansion with its pretentious columns in the front and a detached garage in the back. Jarrett's home was endearingly lopsided, with one corner that seemed out of proportion to the rest of the house—probably a room that had been added on long after the place was originally built. The roof was all crazy angles, hinting at slanted ceilings and interesting attic space. A carport was linked to one side of the house, a screened deck jutted out in the back and there was a generous porch that began within a foot of the front door and wrapped around the opposite corner of the house.

A moment later, she passed beneath the Twisted R sign, her car jostling over the metal grid that kept cattle from wandering out through the entryway between fences. By the time she parked, two dogs had come to greet her. A golden retriever gave an amiable woof as Sierra opened her door; a slightly smaller dog hung back a few feet. It was mostly black with gold paws and a white throat.

"They're friendly," Jarrett called from the porch steps. "But they probably have muddy paws, so if Sunshine looks like she's about to jump on you, tell her no. She'll listen—she just likes to test boundaries."

Sierra grinned down at the retriever, scratching behind her ears. "Fellow boundary-pusher? You and I should get along just fine." She looked up to see Jarrett closing the distance between them with rangy strides. The lighter streaks in his dark hair gleamed in the sun, and the way his jeans fit made her take back any snarky thoughts she'd had about denim.

She spun on her heel toward the back of her car, seizing the distraction of luggage to keep herself from staring at her new boss.

"Can I give you a hand?" he asked from right beside her. Since he was already reaching into the car trunk, the question seemed rhetorical.

She blinked up at him. "You move deceptively fast."

"Long legs." He hefted a suitcase. "We'd just finished lunch when I heard the dogs barking. Have you eaten?"

"I'm good, thanks." She didn't share that her stomach was twisted in knots. Despite the bravado-filled pep talks she'd given herself during the drive, now that she was here, she acknowledged that moving in—even temporarily—was unnerving. She was used to having sole dominion over things like the television remote and the thermostat. Sharing a living space would be an adjustment, no matter who her roommates were. How much would Jarrett's appeal complicate the situation? And then there was Vicki's hostility.

Before Sierra had left the other day, the two women had reached an understanding, but physical therapy was tough. When Vicki was in pain, Sierra would be an easy target for anger. It came with the territory. Sierra was accustomed to dealing with a range of emotions from her patients. But usually she was able to retreat home at the end of a long day and leave the stress of a contrary client behind. Now the contrary client would be sitting across from her at the dinner table.

Good thing I like a challenge.

She passed a large duffel bag to Jarrett, appreciating the ripple of muscles in his forearm as he resituated everything he was carrying. Once they were both loaded down like a couple of pack mules, she followed him up the porch stairs and into the blessedly air-conditioned house. September wasn't as brutal as July or August had been, but the Texas heat was still enough to make her regret the short-sleeved sweater she wore.

They went through the entry hall and past the study, kitchen and Vicki's room. At the end of the hall was a living room decorated in Southwest tones and worn but comfy-looking furniture. A spiral staircase in the far corner led to the second story.

Jarrett flashed a sheepish look over his shoulder. "It's a bit of a climb."

She gave a one-shouldered shrug to show she didn't mind. "It'll help keep me fit."

His gaze swept over her body, and for a second,

she thought he might say something. But he turned around without further comment.

The steps were narrow, and she had to concentrate on not letting her luggage scuff up the walls. At the top, Jarrett gave her the lay of the land. "That's the master bedroom, and that one is—was—Vicki's." He ducked his gaze, his tone flat. They both knew it would be a long time before Vicki Ross climbed those stairs again. "I'm at the other end of the hall, along with the guest room where you'll be."

He gestured for her to go ahead, and Sierra chuckled as she got her first good look at her room—the Island of Misfit Furniture. If she had to guess, she'd say that anytime a room in the house had been remodeled and there was a perfectly good piece of furniture they hadn't wanted to get rid of, it had been shoved in here. The king-size bed was too big for the space. The pink vanity in the corner had probably been Vicki's when she was twelve. The brass headboard was unlike any she'd seen before, a series of whimsical curlicues that curved around the edges of the bed, hugging the mattress.

A few steps into the room, Jarrett had to duck. Because of how the roof slanted down at the edge of the house, there were places where she could probably touch the ceiling if she stood on her toes.

Jarrett frowned. "I haven't been in here since I helped Mom move that old wardrobe. I forgot how claustrophobic it is."

"Not so claustrophobic when you're five foot one."

He set down a suitcase. "Would you rather stay in my parents' room? With as little as we're paying you, the least we could do is offer you comfortable accommodations."

She wasn't her mother, who insisted she couldn't sleep in sheets with less than an eight hundred thread count. "I like the funky vibe. And the wardrobe reminds me of one of my favorite books when I was a kid." Stifling the urge to climb inside and look for magical portals, she turned and ran her hand over the lacy vintage comforter. As long as the mattress was comfortable, even Muriel would have to call this bed luxurious. It was freaking huge. Sierra sat on the edge, bouncing slightly to test it. "This bed's almost too big for one person."

There was a sudden heat in his gaze that made her skin prickle. He looked away, but not before she realized his mind was in a different place than hers. *Great start to the first day—telling your boss you don't want to sleep alone.* Now he was staring fixedly at the wall, as if embarrassed by his wayward thoughts.

She stood, brazening through the moment by making a joke of it. "You don't mind if I host wild orgies on my nights off, do you?"

For a split second, he didn't react. But then his lips quirked in a slow smile. "Orgies, huh? Call me old-fashioned, but I think if one guy can't make you happy, he's not doing it right."

Her heart clutched—not at the outrageous teasing, which she'd started, but at how that grin transformed his face. In town, Kate Sullivan had called Jarrett a charmer. The word didn't fully capture the wicked glint in his eyes or the thrill Sierra got from having coaxed a playful moment. She'd already been drawn to Jarrett more than was appropriate, given their circumstances, but now that she knew about that danger-ously tempting smile and his sense of humor?

For the first time since they'd met, she was the one who lowered her gaze. "I should get settled in," she said, striving for an efficient, professional tone. "The sooner I unpack, the faster I can start helping Vicki."

He flinched. "Vicki. Of course. I'll…see you at dinner."

With that, he was out the door. She honestly didn't know if she was sorry to see him go or relieved.

AT THE RISK of being overly optimistic, Sierra thought that her first hour of PT with Vicki had gone quite well. The young woman hadn't made a single bitchy comment. Granted, she was glaring as if she wanted to kick Sierra's ass, but the good news was, if she ever managed to achieve that, Sierra would know she'd done her job even better than anticipated.

They'd wrapped up a set of exercises, and Vicki was glowering over the top of the water Sierra had handed her.

Sierra slid one of the chairs away from the kitchen table and spun it around, straddling it. "Did your post-surgery therapist talk to you about imagery?"

"No, but my Freshman Lit teacher did. Want to dis-cuss symbolism in 'The Yellow Wallpaper'?"

"I'm talking about positive thinking and having a mental picture of exactly what you want to accom-plish, something specific and concrete." At Vicki's disdainful look, Sierra added, "There have been ac-tual medical studies concluding that imagery can help accelerate the healing process."

"So your clinical approach is for me to close my eyes and chant 'I think I can, I think I can'?"

Well, it had been too much to hope that Vicki's sarcasm was cured forever. "Yeah," Sierra drawled, matching the young woman's scathing tone, "that's exactly what I said. To hell with the carefully researched exercises and the grueling muscle stretches. Let's just hold hands and hope for the best."

The corner of Vicki's lips twitched. "I'm not holding your hand."

"You will if I tell you to," Sierra said mildly. "You're missing the big picture—everything I do is for your benefit. My only goal here is to help *you* make progress." Her only primary goal, anyway. She had secondary objectives of figuring out her future after Cupid's Bow and repressing her attraction to Jarrett. "Look, Vicki, try to keep an open mind and trust that I have the experience to do my job well."

When she didn't respond, Sierra decided to take the silence as acquiescence.

"All right," she continued, "we want to come up with a specific image that you can focus on during sessions, something that will help keep you motivated when you want to quit."

Anger flashed in Vicki's brown eyes. "I'm not a quitter."

"Good. Me neither. So let's harness our collective stubbornness and work together. What is it that you want?"

"To walk again. Without a walker or crutches or anything that makes me feel—" She shook her head fiercely, unwilling to voice her frustration and fear.

"You'll get there," Sierra promised. "Not all the

way there in the three weeks we have, but eventually. But if you could walk right now, no limitations, what would you most want to be doing? Think in terms of sensory details. Build a clear goal in your mind. Hiking outside and feeling the warmth of the sun on your face? Strolling through your favorite store and looking for great sales items?"

"Dancing with Aaron." A smile lit her face. "Aaron Dunn is my boyfriend. There's a dance hall near campus that we love to visit. Aaron's a great dancer. He was teaching me how to jitterbug before last semester ended."

"Perfect. So close your eyes and imagine everything—the song you're listening to, the clothes you're wearing, the smell of beer—er, Aaron's cologne," she amended for her underage client. "Got it?"

Vicki nodded.

"Then let's get to work."

Chapter Six

Jarrett came in through the mudroom that connected the carport and the kitchen. As he pulled off his boots, he heard the sound of female voices arguing on the other side of the door. *Damn.* Maybe it had been irresponsible of him to leave Sierra and Vicki alone all afternoon, but there was so much that needed to be done on the ranch.

Plus, exercising the horses being boarded at the Twisted R and preparing soil for fall crops kept him almost busy enough to avoid picturing Sierra Bailey on that massive bed upstairs.

He groaned, wondering if he had time for a cold shower before he helped negotiate a truce between the women in the kitchen. But then Sierra laughed, a rich throaty sound, and he realized that the bickering he'd overheard was good-natured, not spiteful. He couldn't make out Sierra's words, but whatever she said made Vicki snicker, too.

He froze, trying to recall the last time he'd heard his sister laugh. Amusement had been in short supply since her accident. He'd been confident Sierra could help facilitate his sister's physical rehabilitation, but he hadn't expected that, in one short day, she could help Vicki rediscover joy, too. Gratitude struck him full in the chest. Hearing Vic sound happy, even for an instant, highlighted just how miserable and withdrawn she'd been. He wanted his lighthearted sister back, the one who had a bright future ahead of her and thought her big brother hung the moon.

Then be that guy, her hero, not the jerk who jokes about sexual prowess with the hired help.

Right. No more flirting with Sierra. That moment up in her room had been an anomaly, not proof that he was slipping back into his old habits.

Filled with renewed purpose, he opened the door and entered the kitchen. The door to the walk-in pantry was wide open, and Vicki sat in front of it, craning her head to read some of the cans and boxes on the top shelf from her wheelchair.

Sierra stood at the kitchen counter, writing in a spiral notebook. She spared a quick glance in his direction. "Hey, cowboy. Have a good afternoon milking cows and—"

"They're beef cows," Vicki corrected her. "Not dairy."

"Alrighty." Sierra tried again. "Have a good afternoon herding dogies and riding the range or whatever it is you do?"

Vicki snorted. "You've never spent time on a ranch before, have you?"

"Nah. I'm a fan of civilization—places you can find with GPS, towns with movie theaters that show more than one movie."

"I think the Cupid's Bow Cinema is up to three films at a time," Jarrett defended his hometown. "Although, they might all be from last year. What are you ladies up to?" he asked, crossing the kitchen to get a cup out of the cabinet.

"Grocery list," Sierra said. "I have an exciting Saturday night ahead of meal-planning. It's vital that Vicki gets lots of vitamin D and calcium right now. Meat's important, too, so I'm relieved she's not a vegetarian."

Contemplating a bleak, steakless existence, Jarrett made a face of reflexive terror. "We come from a long line of carnivores."

"Except for softhearted Aunt Pat," Vicki interjected. "She used to help her dad take care of their cows and got too attached. Now she's— What do you call those people who don't eat meat except for seafood?"

"Pescatarian," Sierra supplied.

Vicki snapped her fingers. "Right. But Uncle Gus got her a saltwater aquarium for Christmas, so seafood might be out now, too."

"Fish would be a good staple for your recovery diet," Sierra said. She turned toward Jarrett. "I already went over some options with Vicki. She said she likes trout. That sound okay to you?"

He nodded.

"Have an opinion on mushrooms?"

"I'm not picky." That statement could sum up a lot about his life—big appetite but not a man of discerning tastes.

"Wish the same was true of your sister," Sierra grumbled. "She shot down half the suggestions on my list."

"You tried to get me to eat liver!" Vicki made gagging noises.

"It's high in vitamin D."

"I think you mean high in grossness."

"Well, stay on my good side," Sierra warned, "or it'll be liver seven days a week."

Vicki's eyes widened. "Wait…you have a good side?"

Jarrett didn't mean to laugh, but an errant chuckle escaped. Poking his head in the refrigerator, he reached for the pitcher of water and hoped Sierra hadn't noticed. He didn't want to incur her wrath and end up with an endless banquet of liver lunches and dinners. When he risked glancing in her direction, he found her with her hands on her hips, her posture drawing his attention to her slim waist and the full curve of her hips. Recalling his vow not to be *that Jarrett* anymore, he immediately raised his gaze to her face.

Despite her mock frown, humor danced in her eyes. "Trust me, when my bad side comes out, you'll know the difference."

And just what does it take to entice Sierra Bailey to be bad? The flirtatious words hovered on the tip of his tongue. With the uncharacteristically light mood in the kitchen, it would be so easy to tease her, to fall into the trademark banter he'd used to make time with half the single women in the county.

His grip on the pitcher handle tightened. Hadn't he reminded himself he was no longer that guy only seconds ago? Being in Sierra's presence made it difficult to remember his noble intentions. For weeks, he'd been staying out of town, away from the usual places he frequented, in order to avoid temptation. But now one of the most alluring women he'd ever met was under his roof.

His sense of self-preservation urged him to get out of the house. "I just remembered—I told some buddies I'd try to meet up with them tonight. I can help you make dinner, show you where everything is if you'd like, but after that—"

"You go on." Sierra waved a dismissive hand. "I'm sure Vicki can talk me through everything I need to know."

He nodded, looking to his sister for confirmation.

Her eyes were dark pools of disappointment. Her playful manner was gone, her shoulders slumped. Crap. Vicki hadn't exactly been clamoring for his company lately. It hadn't even crossed his mind that she might want him to stick around for the evening. *I'm doing this for you, Vic.* Staying away from Sierra would help him keep the promise he'd made to his sister.

"Unless you need me to stay?" he asked his sister cautiously.

"No, it's fine. Go. *One* of us should have a social life." Her tone was brittle, on the verge of cracking.

Jarrett rocked back on his heels. The last thing he'd wanted was to upset her. Should he stay after all? Ten minutes ago, Vicki had been laughing; now her expression was grim. *Leave. You've already done enough damage here.*

THE ONLY TRUE bar in Cupid's Bow, not counting the drink counters at the bowling alley or dance hall, was The Neon Arrow. The house specialty was cold beer at a decent price. As he crossed the gravel parking lot, mushier than usual after heavy August rains, Jarrett wondered how long he could nurse a single beer. At his size, he held his liquor well, but ever since Vicki's accident, he never got behind the wheel with more than one drink in him.

After the time it had taken him to shower, change and make the drive, it was fully dark outside. Inside the Arrow, the light wasn't much brighter. Townspeople sat at dimly lit tables or stood gathered around one of the three pool tables in the back half of the little building. He scanned the room halfheartedly for friends, not sure that he was the best company right now. Considering his mood, perhaps it would be better to—

"Long time, no see, stranger." A sudden clap on Jarrett's back made him realize solitude might not be an option.

He turned to see firefighter and longtime friend Will Trent. "Hey."

"Good to see you out and about. Finally. I was starting to seriously consider rounding up my brothers and physically dragging you off the ranch."

"Yeah. Well. Been a rough few months."

"I know." For a moment, grave understanding replaced Will's smile. "How 'bout I buy you a beer to celebrate your being back in circulation?"

"Deal." Jarrett wasn't sure how much circulating he wanted to do, but he could use the drink.

As they headed through the crowd toward the bar, one of the blonde Carmichael sisters kissed Will on the cheek. "Find me if you have time for a game of pool later," she said. "After that bet I lost last week, I want a rematch."

"Same stakes?" Will asked.

Her only answer was a naughty grin.

They made it about three feet when a brunette

punched Will on the arm. "You missed your chance," she angrily declared. "I'm here with Grady Breelan. I am officially *done* waiting by my phone for you to call!" She flounced into the crowd before Will could respond.

"Who was that?" Jarrett asked. "And when did you become the local heartbreaker?" Up until July, that had been Jarrett's title. Will Trent had always been a one-woman man; he'd dated his high school sweetheart for years, then proposed to her. But she'd jilted him before the wedding.

"That was..." Will paused, pursing his lips. "Denise."

"Oh, right. Denise Baker." He should have realized that sooner—after all, they'd gone out briefly. *Very briefly.* He was lucky she hadn't socked him on the arm, too. "I didn't recognize her with short hair."

The line at the bar was considerable, and Will jerked his head toward a nearby high-top table. "We'll probably get service quicker if we sit down and let a waitress take our orders."

That proved accurate when a young woman in a denim vest showed up and asked what she could get them to drink. She was pretty in a freckled, pixie way, but she hardly looked old enough to work in a bar. If Jarrett had run into her on the street, he would have assumed she was Vicki's age. Or younger.

"Will." Her eyes warmed at the sight of the firefighter, and she resituated her tray, leaning in to give him a one-armed hug. "How are you doin' tonight?"

"Just fine, Amy. You know Jarrett Ross?"

"Not personally, but I've seen him in the rodeo ring. You're practically a celebrity," she said to Jarrett. "You riding next month over in Brazoria County?"

"No." Too bad Jarrett didn't have a drink yet. Beer, water, soda—he didn't care. His throat was painfully dry. He used to brag all the time about his wins, but now talking about rodeo made him feel as if he were gargling with sawdust. "I'm taking some time off."

Her laugh had a sad edge to it. "Wish I could afford some time off every now and then."

"You still working two jobs?" Will asked.

"Three, but who's counting?" She gave herself a shake, plastering on a bright smile. "Y'all aren't here to listen to me whine. It's Saturday night! You should be having fun—have a little extra for me, okay?" With that, she scooted off to retrieve their drinks. She returned with a couple of frosty longnecks wrapped in napkins.

When Will tried to tip her more than the drinks cost, she protested. "You're a doll, Will Trent, but I'm no charity case."

"The money's not for you—it's for that baby of yours. Give him a hug for me."

With a sigh, she tucked the cash into the zippered pouch she wore belted around her waist. Then she kissed Will on the same cheek that the blonde had.

After Amy was gone, Jarrett asked, "You two aren't...?"

Will sat back in his chair, his expression appalled. "Hell no. I think Amy was a junior or sophomore when my younger brother graduated. She's just a kid. With a kid of her own." Frowning, he watched her clear empty bottles from the next table. "Her apartment got hit by lightning in a storm last month, and I helped put out the fire. Frankly, I'm almost glad it happened."

Jarrett's eyebrows shot up. "Because it broke up the monotony of a slow week?"

"Because Amy had to temporarily move in with her mom while the damage was being repaired. Living at home helped her break things off with her loser boyfriend. The guy's bad news. Cole's pretty sure he deals drugs but hasn't been able to prove it yet." Will's older brother was the town sheriff. "The night of the fire, Amy had a bruise on her arm she claimed was from banging into the kitchen counter while trying to heat a bottle. Except, the bruise was in the shape of fingers."

The thought of a woman being hurt made Jarrett ill. "She have a dad or big brothers to look out for her?" Maybe someone needed to have a conversation with her ex.

"Just a self-appointed, honorary brother tipping her with fives and tens when I can."

Even though Will had called the waitress a "kid," as a mother providing for her child, she was more of a grown-up than Jarrett was. He would be thirty in a few years, but up until July, he'd been dancing through life with no real responsibility.

"Speaking of siblings," Will said, "how's your sister doing?"

"She's…" He took a long swallow of beer, unsure how to answer. Certainly Vicki had improved since her days in the hospital, when she'd been pale, listless and unable to even sit up. Sierra was hoping to transition her to a walker, and he was grateful for every bit of progress. Yet it was still difficult to believe that the exuberant girl who'd always taken the front porch stairs two at a time couldn't climb any stairs at all. If going in through the carport hadn't already been an option, they would have needed to build a ramp for her.

Then there was the damage done to their relationship. How long would it take to rebuild the trust and camaraderie? When he'd impulsively said he was going out for the evening, he'd hoped Sierra and Vicki would continue to bond in his absence—maybe watch one of those mushy movies that Vicki and his mom always sniffled through but that made Jarrett restless for the end credits. But she'd been so sullen when he left, glaring with unspoken accusation. Did she think he'd pawned her off on Sierra so that he could pick up a woman and make up for lost time?

"Damn," Will said softly. "That bad?"

"We hired a therapist to stay at the ranch for a few weeks. She seems to really know her stuff, so maybe Vicki's next big milestone is right around the corner." He wondered if his smile looked as fake as it felt.

"Local buzz was that you were hiring Lucy Aldridge."

"My parents and I discussed that, but we went in a different direction." Jarrett thought about Sierra's red-gold hair and frequent warnings not to incur her wrath. *Very, very different.* He just hoped it wasn't a direction he would regret.

SIERRA ENTERED THE kitchen bright and early Monday morning. *Technically,* she thought, stifling a yawn, *dark and early.*

She was greeted by the heavenly aroma of coffee and resounding silence. The mug and cereal bowl in the sink attested that Jarrett had been there, but apparently he'd already headed out to tackle ranch chores. She'd barely seen him since his abrupt departure from the house Saturday. Yesterday, he'd taught riding lessons for most of the afternoon and told them not to wait on him for dinner. Sierra almost felt as if he were avoiding her.

Which makes you either paranoid or conceited. He could just as easily be avoiding Vicki, pained to see his sister in a handicapped state. Or maybe Sierra was overthinking the matter and he was just really busy. After all, the Twisted R was over a hundred acres, and Jarrett was taking care of everything by himself. If his daily schedule were leisurely, he wouldn't have needed to hire her in the first place.

Hours later, as she was fixing lunch, he came in through the side door off the kitchen, which made her feel silly about her unfounded suspicions.

"Hope you're hungry," she said, "because—"

"I am, actually, but I'll grab a bite in town. I'm making a run to the feed store, then picking up some lumber." Then he was gone as quickly as he'd appeared.

Apparently, he hadn't even taken the time to say goodbye to his sister before leaving the ranch. When Sierra and Vicki sat down to eat, the girl barely touched her homemade soup or grilled cheese sandwich; she was too busy glancing at the door every few seconds. Obviously, she'd expected—hoped?—that Jarrett would join them.

Sierra followed her gaze. "If you're waiting on your brother, he had some errands to run."

"Oh." Vicki's shoulders slumped.

Sierra bit the inside of her lip, wondering if he knew how disappointed his sister was not to spend more time with him. "I guess the ranch keeps him pretty busy," she said, hoping to ease the sting of his absence. "Seems like a lot of hard work."

"Yeah." Vicki dragged a spoon through her soup, making little swirls in the broth. "Must be nice."

It was one thing to envy Jarrett a night on the town, but was Vicki really jealous about the hours he spent patching fences or baling hay? *She's bored out of her skull.* Sierra was not a dull person, but not even her companionship could replace the entire sophomore class at Vicki's university.

There were gaps in the nineteen-year-old's day. As much as Sierra liked to goad her patients into giving maximum effort, overdoing the exercises would only complicate recovery. Between sets, Vicki had to take it easy. Physically, anyway. They needed to find her something more mentally challenging than daytime TV.

It would be best if Vicki had her own project during the hours when Sierra was tracking down job leads, cleaning or grocery shopping. The idea was for the two women to work as a team, not spend so much time stuck in each other's company that they got sick of each other. Maybe Vicki could take some online courses to help catch up to her classmates? Not that Sierra could authorize such an expense. She needed to discuss options with Jarrett, maybe tonight after dinner.

And if he kept making himself scarce? Then she'd just have to track him down.

Chapter Seven

Sierra squinted into the dusk, her resolve momentarily faltering. Were there snakes out there? She had no idea. But cow patties were inevitable.

So watch where you step. She was carrying a flashlight in one hand and a bagged roast beef sandwich in the other. Jarrett had missed dinner for the third night in a row; when it had become clear that he wouldn't be there, Vicki had looked as if she might cry. It was time Sierra and her employer had a chat.

Randomly wandering one hundred and fifty acres in search of him would be a fool's errand, but the light spilling from a huge barn let her know where she could find him. Marching down the porch steps, she headed in that direction and tried not to think about the coyote howls she'd heard in the distance last night. At least, she hoped they were suitably distant.

The dogs trailed along beside her, probably drawn by the smell of roast beef, and she was comforted by their presence. "You'd let me know if there was anything in the dark to worry about, right, Sunshine?"

The retriever perked up at the sound of her name.

"If the two of you keep me safe from critters," Sierra

promised the dogs, "there are yummy scraps of roast beef in your future."

Despite the dimness of the evening around her, it wasn't so dark that the stars were truly visible yet. She bet they were spectacular this far from any city, and she made a mental note to stargaze one night. Might as well take advantage of the view before she returned to her regularly scheduled urban life. Who knew when she'd ever fall this far off the beaten path again? She heard a horse whinny and grimaced. *Definitely* not *my kind of place.*

There weren't any horses in the fenced paddock outside the barn. Vicki had said something yesterday about them spending daylight hours in the pastures and being stabled at night. Sierra could tolerate being near one if it was safely on the other side of a stall door. Still, when another horse nickered in reply to the first, she felt a phantom pain along her spine, tightening her lower back and making it momentarily difficult to move forward. *Screw that. You are Sierra Bailey.*

Shoulders squared, she stomped into the barn with more gusto than tact. "Are you avoiding me?"

Several equine heads turned her way, their long faces poking over stall doors, their eyes dark and huge. She swallowed hard.

A stall door to her left swung open, and Jarrett emerged, looking perplexed. "One of the mares we board is a little high-strung," he said softly. "As a general rule, I encourage people to use calm, soothing voices."

"Sorry," she said, matching his tone. She held up the plastic bag as a peace offering. "I brought you some dinner. We weren't sure when you'd make it back to the house."

His gaze zeroed in hungrily on the sandwich. "Thank you. I was so busy giving these guys hay for the night I didn't realize I was starving." After latching the stall door closed, he stripped off the pair of work gloves he'd been wearing and reached forward to take the food.

Then he walked toward the back of the stable, gesturing with a head tilt for her to follow. There was a small wooden bench built into the far wall. She took a seat while he washed his hands at a sink around the corner. Was there enough room for him to join her? They'd have to sit very close, a prospect that seemed simultaneously tantalizing and ill-advised. She was glad when he sat a few feet away on a bale of hay.

"What's this about me avoiding you?" he asked, unwrapping his sandwich.

She really should learn diplomacy someday. "Well, uh, I've been here three nights, and in that time you haven't come to the house for supper once."

"You do understand these horses don't groom and feed themselves, right?" He looked annoyed. And sweaty. And far more comfortable in his own skin than the reserved man who'd first interviewed her. In this setting, he—

What is wrong with you? She didn't like barns or horses or the smell of hay. It was completely illogical that she'd be drawn to a cowboy with scuffed boots and a streak of dirt across the upper thigh of his jeans. Realizing that her gaze had dropped to his lap, she jerked her head up, feeling as twitchy as that mare he'd mentioned.

"Let me start over," Sierra said. "I approached this

wrong because I was a little jumpy about walking in the dark and—"

"Maybe you should've stayed inside the well-lit house."

"Trust me, I'm all for well-lit houses and indoor plumbing and air-conditioning. I wouldn't venture out among the mosquitoes and cow pies without good reason. And Vicki is my reason." She took a deep breath, reminding herself of her purpose. Best to focus on her patient's well-being, not Jarrett's denim-clad thighs.

He leaned forward, his expression tense. "Is she okay? Did something—"

"Nothing happened. I just needed to talk to you about her frame of mind. Maybe this isn't the ideal time and place, but for two people who live in the same house, we don't seem to run into each other much," she said wryly. Before he could turn defensive, she added, "I'm sure that's because the ranch keeps you so busy. But your sister..." She recalled Vicki's haunted expression at dinner as she once again spent an entire meal staring at the door instead of eating. "Are the two of you close?"

He stiffened. "Did she say something? About me?"

"Not specifically."

"Oh." His gaze dropped to his sandwich, but he didn't take another bite. If the Ross siblings didn't start eating more, Sierra was going to get a complex about her cooking. "There's a pretty big gap in our ages."

Was that his way of explaining why he and his sister didn't spend more time together? Sierra had dealt with her fair share of evasive answers from patients who didn't want to admit that they'd been slacking off; she knew guilty undertones when she heard them. "Age difference aside, she seems like she really misses you."

That got his attention. His eyes lit with something almost like hope, but then he shook his head. "I doubt it. And, as I said, the ranch keeps me busy."

"Are you one of those people who get uncomfortable around anyone who has a handicap?" she asked impatiently. "Because Vicki will be in that wheelchair for—"

"I assist with equine therapy for disabled kids and adults, and you don't know what you're talking about."

Oh, good—she'd misjudged her boss *and* angered him. She could just apologize and leave, except that retreating wouldn't do anything to improve Vicki's situation. She took a fortifying breath, trying not to wrinkle her nose at the prevailing horsey smell, and gave her best attempt at a conciliatory smile. "One of the things your sister did say was that you're lucky to have so much to do. I think she's bored and feeling a little useless."

"Of course she is." He rubbed his forehead with the heel of his hand. "She should be at college, not cooped up in the house. This is all my—"

He didn't have to finish the sentence for Sierra to understand that he blamed himself. Sympathy tugged at her. She'd been told Vicki was driving alone and had been hit by a drunk driver. Did Jarrett have any rational reason to feel guilty? Then again, emotions didn't always adhere to logic. This inappropriate impulse she was feeling right now to go hug him, for instance...

She cleared her throat. "Is there some kind of project we can give her? Something truly beneficial, not busywork that makes it seem like we pity her." Patronizing her would only court the young woman's resentment. "Do you know I've heard three different people in town call her 'poor Vicki'?" Earlier, Sierra had wondered if an online class would be good for her patient. Now she reconsidered. Vicki needed something less solitary, something that would demonstrate to the people of Cupid's Bow—and to herself—that wheelchair or not, she was a smart, capable woman.

Jarrett scowled. "Surely no one would be dumb enough to say that to her face?"

"Whether they do or not, the sentiment is there. What can we do to change it? Is there some kind of local charity she could volunteer with, or—"

"There's the Harvest Day Festival," he said. "It's an annual event the last weekend in September. Basic fall celebration—hayrides, face paintings, pumpkin-carving contest. My friend Will and I were just talking about it the other night. The place where we normally hold it is out because of construction on the new courthouse in downtown Cupid's Bow."

She managed not to snicker at the idea of a "downtown" in a place that probably had only four city blocks.

"They've relocated it to a park, so—according to Will's soon-to-be sister-in-law, Kate—it's taking more planning than normal since they have to refigure the layout. Maybe Vicki could help? She's lived here her whole life and knows that park like the back of her hand. Or, the committee's always making calls asking for different donations and recruiting people to emcee the square dance or judge the Harvest Queen contest. Vicki can phone call with the best of them."

His mouth tilted upward in a half grin. "Trust me, I've seen some of her cell-phone bills."

"This sounds really promising," Sierra said, feeling a burst of optimism. "Any idea who we'd talk to about getting her signed up?"

"Kate's on the committee, but Becca Johnston is probably running it. That woman is in charge of half the stuff in town. Start with her. But if she says anything to you about a bachelor auction, my answer is no. Unequivocally, emphatically *no*. I'm still not sure how the hell she talked me into that at the Watermelon Festival."

"You were in a bachelor auction?" Had he worn his standard uniform of jeans and boots, or had it been one of those charity events where they paraded the bachelors in tuxes? She studied him from beneath discreetly lowered lashes, trying to imagine the tall cowboy in a tuxedo. *Ross. Jarrett Ross.*

"Once. Against my better judgment. Never again." As if to underscore the finality of his decision, he stood. "Thanks for the sandwich, but if I don't get back to work, I'll be here all night."

"Right. Sorry."

"Don't be. You came out here with Vicki's best interests at heart, and that means a lot to me. *She* means a lot to me." He expelled a heavy breath. "To answer your earlier question, we were close. Before."

"You will be again." That was a rather ballsy statement, considering she didn't even know the cause of their rift. But Sierra's entire career—pretty much her life—was based on the belief that wounds could be healed, given sufficient time and effort. "Try to join us for dinner tomorrow?"

His silvery eyes held hers for a long moment. "I'll try."

Well. It was a start.

She took a few steps forward, subtly glancing around to see if the dogs were nearby. It was a lot darker out now than it had been when she'd arrived, and she wouldn't mind the canine escort back to the house.

"Everything okay?" Jarrett asked from behind her.

"Absolutely. Just fine. I—"

A black-and-white horse suddenly poked its head through the stall, as if curious about their conversation, and Sierra jumped, flinching away from the giant nose and flaring nostrils.

"That's Panda, Vicki's favorite. My sister has her spoiled and now Pan expects everyone to bring her carrots or pear slices. You can pet her," he encouraged, reaching up to pat the horse's neck.

"Oh, no. Thanks." She would have moved even farther away, except that would only bring her closer to the stall on the opposite side and the beast lumbering therein. Why did horses have to be so *big*? If only the Twisted R stabled ponies. Maybe those cute, super-shaggy ones. She was reasonably certain those wouldn't alarm her.

Jarrett quirked an eyebrow, looking amused. "Let me guess—you've never been around horses before."

"Actually, I have." She kneaded the muscles of her lower back, as if she could rub away past pain. "I... fell off one." Technically, she was thrown. More arrogant than experienced, she'd decided she was ready to try jumping the horse. Her mount had not agreed, balking at the last minute.

"A bad fall?"

She managed not to shudder at the memory. "Yeah."

His eyes widened. "The day I hired you, you told Vicki you'd suffered a spinal injury. Was—"

"Yeah."

"I'm sorry you were hurt," he said, stepping away from Panda, "but I respect the hell out of what you do—building from a painful experience of your own to help other people. It's… Will you laugh at me if I call you heroic?"

She was used to combating disapproval about her methods or her personality; Jarrett's earnest praise left her discomfited. Beneath his admiring gaze, her cheeks heated. Good grief. Since when did she blush? "Hero's a new one," she joked. "Most people just call me a dictator with a Napoleon complex."

"I'm serious. Your work *matters*. Some people are so damn selfish, barreling through life with no impact at all on those around them." His mouth twisted, his expression one of sheer disgust. "Except to hurt them."

She didn't know who had wounded Jarrett with self-absorbed actions, but the righteous fury in his eyes almost made her feel sorry for the guilty party. "Well. Thank you," she said awkwardly. She had that same errant impulse to soothe him that she'd had while sitting at the back of the barn, as if she wanted to go hug him.

Stupid. Not one of her brothers would appreciate a sympathetic hug—what made her think the strapping cowboy would? And, if she were being honest with herself, she wasn't sure the urge was that altruistic. Empathy aside, she couldn't deny the feminine thrill that shot through her at the idea of being that close to him, feeling the body sculpted by years of ranch work and rodeos against her own. *Get out of this barn before you start entertaining any trite roll-in-the-hay fantasies.*

With one final nod in his direction, she hurried outside. At the moment, potential critters in the dark weren't nearly as alarming as the pull she felt toward Jarrett Ross.

"YOU'RE GIVING ME the afternoon off?" Vicki narrowed her eyes, regarding Sierra with suspicion. "Why? That's not like you."

Sierra shrugged. Chopping vegetables at the kitchen island provided a convenient excuse to turn away from Vicki's scrutiny. "Even taskmasters take the occasional break to have lunch with their friends."

"*You* have a friend in Cupid's Bow?"

"Kate Sullivan." It was a stroke of luck that the woman had turned out to be on the festival committee. "I met her my first day in town, and she's nice. Which is a welcome change from your company."

"What?" Vicki feigned confusion. "I'm delightful. Ask anyone. You must bring out the worst in me."

Sierra's lips curled in a grin. In some ways, Vicki reminded her of a younger version of herself. She wondered if her patient would take that comparison as a compliment. *Why should she? You're a pain in the ass.* True. But she was a pain with a purpose. When she'd called Kate this morning to ask about the Harvest Day Festival, the woman had said her timing couldn't be more perfect.

"The committee meets every Tuesday at the Smoky Pig for lunch," Kate had told her. "Are you free to join us today?"

Sierra had promptly rearranged her schedule. Jarrett had promised to come to the house for lunch, so he could eat with Vicki while Sierra went into town. She hadn't yet told her patient about the festival idea. This way, if there was no pressing job open for the young woman, she didn't need to know about the rejection or worry that the other members had turned her down because they viewed her as incapable. Besides, while Sierra and her patient had steadily been building a productive relationship, Vicki still had her prickly moods. Sierra would rather present the opportunity as a fait accompli than have Vicki balk at the suggestion.

"As soon as I get lunch prepared for you and your brother, I—"

"Hold that thought," Vicki declared, pulling her cell phone out of her hoodie pocket. Her eyes widened and, by the way her face lit, Sierra knew immediately who the caller was. "Aaron? Wait just a second. I'm taking this in my room," she informed Sierra. Then she rolled herself from the kitchen with speed normally reserved for professional racetracks.

Watching the giddy display of young love, Sierra felt simultaneously charmed and jaded. Had she ever cared about anyone with that much enthusiasm? She'd adored Paul, but in a more…practical way. He was a good person who shared a lot of the same values she did and didn't mind her outspoken nature. But as much as she'd enjoyed spending time with him, she'd never moped if a day passed without his calling. *Well, you weren't nineteen.*

The door to the mudroom creaked open behind her. She turned to find Jarrett tilting his black cowboy hat on his head so he could rub a bead of sweat off his jaw with the sleeve of his T-shirt. Her heart stuttered at the absent male gesture.

She gave herself a mental shake. *What happened to mature and practical?*

"Sierra? You okay?"

She swallowed, trying to bring her thoughts into focus. "Um...don't I look okay?"

He cocked his head, studying her. "You looked... intense."

"Oh. Probably because I'm busy plotting."

"Global domination?"

"Nah. I thought I'd start at the state level and work my way up." She glanced past the kitchen to make sure Vicki was well out of earshot, then lowered her voice. "I'm making lunch for you and your sister, but I won't be staying to eat. Kate Sullivan is picking me up soon. For a festival meeting."

"Great. But why are we whispering?"

"I haven't exactly told Vicki about my brilliant idea yet. Her reactions can be a little...unpredictable. So I'm going with the ethically questionable maxim that it's better to ask forgiveness than permission."

"You're going to volunteer her time without asking her first?"

"That's the plan," she said cheerfully. "Assuming you'll okay my taking a few hours off for the meeting."

"Of course. That actually works out well since I have a lot of office work to catch up on. So I can be in the house while you're gone." He paused. "Wait. You and Kate already arranged for her to come get you."

"Yep."

"But you're just now asking if it's all right. Out of curiosity, what would you have done if I'd said no?"

"Changed your mind." She gave him what she hoped was a winning smile. "I'm a very pushy person."

"I hadn't noticed," he drawled, his expression deadpan. "Do I have time to take a shower before lunch is ready?"

Since they were sharing a bathroom, it was far too easy to picture him in the generously sized shower stall with its clear door and chrome finishing. Annoyed with herself for the undisciplined—and highly erotic—mental images, she snapped, "Make it quick."

He raised an eyebrow at her tone. "Careful, darlin'. You rush a guy, you don't always get the results you deserve."

Heat flooded her. The idea of Jarrett taking his time wasn't any safer to dwell on than the vision of him wearing nothing but a few soapsuds. Whistling under his breath, he left the room. She waited until he'd disappeared around the corner to stick her head in the freezer.

Chapter Eight

"I'm so glad you called me," Kate said as they rolled over the cattle guard and onto the road. "I was already thinking about getting in touch and inviting you to lunch sometime, but I didn't want to be pushy. I know it can take time to settle in."

Sierra pulled a pair of sunglasses out of her purse. "Not much settling to do—I'll only be here three more weeks, give or take."

"And you want to spend part of your short time here involved with the festival? Do they not have cable on the ranch?"

"This isn't an act of boredom so much as me scheming to get Vicki Ross reengaged with the community. My interest in the festival is to get *her* signed up for a job. Will you help me convince the rest of the committee? Vicki's bright and has ample time on her hands."

"Sure. I don't know her well, but she's always struck me as smart and energetic. According to my fiancé, she used to babysit the twins before she left for college. Anyone who can successfully manage Alyssa and Mandy has my respect."

The ride into town didn't take nearly as long as Sierra remembered. It probably helped that she could just enjoy their conversation—which touched on everything from Kate's search for the right wedding dress to college football—instead of worrying about getting lost. Soon, they were parking in a public lot at the end of the picturesque—if unimaginatively named—Main Street.

"From here we walk." Kate grinned. "Which gives me the chance to burn off at least a couple of calories before I stuff my face with barbecue."

They climbed out of the car, greeted by energetic gusts of wind. Sierra's polka-dot skirt whipped around in a breeze perfumed with sweet, earthy scents from the nearby flower shop. Her hair blew in her face, and she regretted not wearing it pulled back.

"When I left Gram's farm," Kate said, "Luke was decorating kites with the girls to fly in the pasture, but with the way it's picking up, this wind might be too strong for them. No clouds yet, but you can tell a storm will be rolling in." Glancing up at the blue sky, she inhaled deeply. "I love that sense of electricity in the air before it rains."

Electricity. Maybe Sierra could blame the impending change in weather for the zing that had gone through her in the kitchen earlier, for the not unpleasant way her skin prickled when she locked eyes with Jarrett. That hum she felt through her body could be some trick of barometric pressure instead of wildly unprofessional lust. *Absolutely...and Santa Claus and unicorns are real, too.* Physical attraction was one thing. If Jarrett were only a hot cowboy, without an intriguing personality to match those mesmerizing silvery eyes, she could ignore her baser instincts. But the chiseled face was paired with gallant protective instincts and his heady admiration for Sierra. He'd labeled her a hero. How was a girl supposed to resist that? And then there were those fleeting, unexpected moments of wicked teasing. If she didn't know better, she would swear he'd been flirting with her before she left.

Careful, darlin'.

Sierra's mother called everyone "darling." The way Muriel said it was impersonal, the verbal equivalent of an air-kiss. But when Jarrett drawled the word, it was rich and beguiling. An invitation.

Consider it an invitation mailed to the wrong address, she told herself. *Whatever you do, don't open it.*

"Wanna be a little bit bad?" Kate asked.

"What?" Sierra jolted, startled by the question. Could people tell just by looking at her what she was thinking? That would make dinner tonight with Vicki and Jarrett extremely awkward.

"Trying on wedding dresses has made me resolve to lose ten pounds," Kate said as she slowed beneath a striped awning and reached for the restaurant door, "but this place has the *best* desserts. I was hoping you'd split one with me after lunch. Then it's only half bad. Which is practically half good."

"So my enabling you would be my good deed for the day?" Sierra grinned. "I like the way you think."

As they walked inside, Sierra pushed her sunglasses up on her head to better see. The wood-paneled walls and exposed railing made the interior of the restaurant dark, but judging by the mouthwatering smell of barbecue, people didn't come here for the decorating.

"We're back there," Kate said, leading Sierra to where three tables had been pushed together to accommodate a group of women, ranging in age from their twenties to over seventy.

"Which one's Becca?" Sierra whispered.

Kate paused, pursing her lips. "I don't see her, which is weird. She's usually the first one here. Although, maybe today is one of the days she's meeting with her contractor. She's about to start substantial house renovations. And woe to the contractor who does not give that woman exactly what she wants."

"Is she really so scary?"

"She's nice, if you get to know her. But she's detail-oriented, with a *very* specific idea of how things should be done, and a little intimidating. Gram calls her ruthlessly efficient." As they reached the table, Kate beamed at the assembled women. "Afternoon, everyone! I brought a new recruit with me—Sierra Bailey."

"Oooh." A brunette seated in the middle flashed a teasing smile. "Fresh blood. Did you warn her what she's in for?"

"I'm actually here on behalf of Vicki Ross," Sierra said. "I've been working with her, and—"

"That poor girl," an older woman murmured.

Nods of agreement followed around the table, making Sierra want to roll her eyes.

"Everything that poor family has been through," a woman with a sleek blond bob said mournfully. "I've been meaning to go out to the ranch and check on Vicki. Maybe take her brother a casserole."

An auburn-haired woman across the table snorted. "That's not all you want to give him."

"Why, Anita Drake! That is so dirty-minded of you. And, also, true." The blonde shrugged apologetically at Sierra. "Jarrett Ross is hot."

No argument here. "Mr. Ross isn't really my concern," she said neutrally. "But I've been working as his sister's live-in physical therapist. I'm pleased to report Vicki's making great progress. Everyone in Cupid's Bow has been so sweet in their concern for her, and she wants to give back to the community. I'm hoping we can find a way for her to help with the festival."

"Which I think is a wonderful idea," Kate seconded. "I—"

"Disaster!" A woman in pearls and a pink sweater set looked up from her glowing phone screen. "Becca just texted me on her way here from the park. There's been minor flooding around the river, and with the additional rain expected this week, entire sections of the park might be underwater for the festival. Ladies, we need a new location immediately!"

"So." Sierra had been quiet for a few minutes after leaving the restaurant, needing time to process. When she finally spoke, they were halfway down the sidewalk. "That was Becca Johnston, huh?"

Kate smiled. "She can be a lot to take when you first meet her."

"I think she's my new hero." Sierra was used to being the bossiest redhead in any room, but the tall strawberry blonde had her beat. The woman was a force of nature. One glare from her and any gossiping or dissension around the table stopped immediately.

"And you haven't seen her at full strength," Kate said. "That was Becca on a preoccupied day."

The committee head had admitted as much, saying that her life was about to be turned upside down with home renovations and she needed the festival problem solved *now*. Kate had offered her grandmother's farm, which Becca dismissed as too small. Another committee member was suggesting they ask a rancher named Brody Davenport when the would-be casserole bearer who'd earlier declared Jarrett hot interrupted to say the Twisted R would be perfect. Apparently, his parents had hosted local events there in years past.

"Done," Becca had decreed. "We'll have it at the Twisted R."

Someone had wondered aloud if they should secure Jarrett's formal permission first, but Becca didn't have time for naysayers. The specifics of the conversation were fuzzy, but Sierra remembered nodding along with Becca's sound reasoning. Yes, they did need a new home for the festival as soon as possible. And hosting the festival at the Twisted R was a perfect way to involve Vicki, who could help work out where all the proposed activities should be situated.

Becca had eyed Sierra, sizing her up. "You don't strike me as the type of woman who takes no for an answer."

"Definitely not."

"Wonderful. Then you're the perfect point person to give Jarrett Ross the good news."

Climbing into Kate's car, Sierra wondered how angry Jarrett would be when he discovered his ranch had been selected without his approval. *On the plus side, at least I didn't sign him up for a bachelor auction.*

WHEN SIERRA ENTERED the house, she was surprised to find Vicki at the kitchen table doing wrist exercises.

"I've been waiting for you to get back! Can we try some chair stands?" Vicki asked. They'd discussed how they were working up to Vicki holding the back of a chair and slowly standing, getting a sense of how much weight she could actually put on her legs.

"Eager. Cooperative." Sierra rocked back on her heels. "Who are you and what have you done with Vicki Ross?"

"Guess who's coming to see me this weekend?" Her face was rosy, and she was practically vibrating with joy in her wheelchair. "Aaron! You were gone when we got off the phone, so I didn't get the chance to tell you, but that's why he called. He's going to skip his afternoon class on Friday and drive to Cupid's Bow as soon as he finishes his calculus test that morning. I can't wait to see him! I want to show him I'm getting stronger."

"Fantastic news." Obviously Sierra wouldn't have to push very hard to keep her patient motivated for the rest of the week. Plus, based on Vicki's glorious mood, today would be the perfect time to tell her that Sierra had volunteered her to help organize the festival.

Over dinner. Sierra had already decided to cook chicken and dumplings—a specialty she'd learned from her mother's housekeeper—to soften up Jarrett. She hoped the meal made him as mellow as it usually did her father and brothers. The three of them could briefly discuss the festival, and then she would change the subject to what to cook while Aaron was here. Vicki would be too excited about the latter to protest the former.

"Will you take me shopping?" Vicki asked. "We have my appointment at the hospital Thursday. Can we go to All That Jazz afterward? I want to buy something special."

"Sounds like a good plan. Kate recommended I check out the boutique while I was in town. Why not make a day of it? Your therapy follow-up, lunch—"

"And the salon!" Vicki fingered the ends of her hair. "Maybe it's time for a new hairstyle. Nothing insanely different, just…a change."

Sierra nodded encouragingly. "Change is good."

"You sound like Jarrett. He always used to say that to justify—"

"To justify what?" Sierra asked, sitting next to Vicki at the table.

"Nothing."

The urge to pry was strong. There were undercurrents between the Ross siblings that Sierra didn't understand. On the one hand, she would swear that they were closer—or, used to be closer—than she'd ever been with her brothers. But the tension between them could be overwhelming. Sierra felt as if she'd wandered into a play during the second act, unsure of the story line. She'd gleaned that Jarrett blamed himself for Vicki's accident. Did Vicki think he was at fault, too? Had they argued about it?

"Jarrett promised he'd be joining us for dinner," Sierra said.

"Okay." Vicki stared at her hand as she wiggled her fingers. She had the appearance of someone trying very hard to look as if she didn't care.

"Did the two of you talk much at lunch?" Sierra prodded.

"I told him Aaron will be visiting and that we don't need chaperones looking over our shoulders every three minutes." She met Sierra's gaze. "I want to keep up with my therapy so I can be walking on campus again as soon as possible, but when we're not working—"

"Make myself scarce. Got it. I promise not to cramp your style."

Vicki grinned. "You're not completely heinous."

"Wow. Mind if I steal that for my résumé? Sierra Bailey, Licensed Physical Therapist, Not Completely Heinous. The job offers should come pouring in."

"You really don't know where you're going after this?"

"Not a clue." Which she was trying not to let terrify her. Now that she'd secured a project for Vicki, she needed to ramp up her efforts at looking for a job. If nothing else, maybe mailing cover letters and résumés would keep her too busy to have inappropriate thoughts about her boss.

"We know some rodeo riders who bust up their ribs and get concussions and stuff. Maybe you'll decide to stay and open a practice in Cupid's Bow."

"Doubtful," Sierra scoffed. "Cute town, but more a detour for me than a destination." It was not her kind of place.

Although, after an afternoon of laughing with Kate and enjoying scrumptious food, it was hard to remember why not.

"If that tastes as good as it smells, you may be in the wrong profession." Jarrett appeared at the edge of the kitchen, barefoot in a white T-shirt and a pair of jeans fraying at the hems. Closing his eyes, he inhaled, a look of blissful anticipation settling over his face. "My plan was to keep working in the office until you called me for dinner, but I haven't been able to focus on anything for the past ten minutes except the wonderful smells wafting down the hall. What are you making?"

"Chicken and dumplings, roasted green beans, spinach salad with homemade bacon vinaigrette. And there's an apple cobbler in the oven."

"Mmm. Is this to say thank-you for having the afternoon off? Because if that's the case, you can take off every afternoon."

"Oh. Nice," Vicki said as she rolled into the room. "So we've decided that me regaining use of my legs ranks slightly below fresh-baked apple cobbler?"

Jarrett whirled around, the color draining from his face. "Of course not. I—"

"Relax." She sighed, her expression unreadable. "I was just giving you crap. You used to be able to tell when I was kidding," she added, her voice barely audible.

The pained silence that fell across the kitchen like a shadow made Sierra's heart ache. She cleared her throat. "If you two are finished busting each other's chops, how about you make yourselves useful and set the table? Vicki, you can get the silverware."

Dinner really did smell fantastic, but, once it was served, no one dug in with much gusto. Sierra was still pleasantly stuffed from a big lunch and the carrot cake Kate had talked her into sharing. Five minutes ago, Jarrett had been starving. Now he kept casting his sister searching looks while she mostly stared at her plate, lost in thought. So much for the food putting them in a jovial mood that would make them receptive to her festival news.

Might as well get this over with. Sierra set her fork down and turned to Jarrett. "You remember my saying that sometimes it's easier to ask forgiveness than permission?"

He hesitated with a forkful of dumpling to his mouth. "Yes."

"Good. I need you to forgive me. I told the Harvest Day Festival committee that they could hold the festival here at the ranch."

"You *what*?" Surprisingly, this didn't come from Jarrett but from Vicki, who then burst out laughing.

For his part, Jarrett looked as if he didn't know what to say. He gaped at her, unblinking. "Huh. Well, you did warn me that was your approach. I just thought you were planning to ambush her with it." He jerked his chin toward Vicki, who sobered quickly.

"Wait, what? Ambush me how?"

An equal opportunity ambusher, Sierra turned to beam at the other Ross sibling. "You're going to be working with Kate Sullivan to figure out where to put everything on the ranch. They had a rough plan drawn out for the park, but since the creek's flooded and more rain is coming…" She faltered under the combined weight of their stares. "Look, guys, the meeting didn't go quite the way I imagined. I went with Kate hoping to find Vicki something to do so you're not cooped up in the house and bored. You were envying Jarrett his ranch chores the other day—chores that involve mucking horse poo out of stalls! Working on the festival has to beat shoveling poo, right?"

Vicki's lips twitched as if she were holding back a laugh. "Manure," she corrected her.

"Potato, potahto." Sierra waved a hand. Sensing that she'd appeased Vicki, she turned to Jarrett. "I had no idea they were going to need a different venue. The flooding problem came up and someone suggested the Twisted R, which Becca Johnston agreed was the best solution. After that, it's kind of a blur, but everything she said made so much sense, and she said she was trusting me to clear it with you and…"

"Oh my gosh!" Vicki's eyes twinkled. "You got Becca'd."

"Becca'd?" They'd made the head of the committee a verb?

Jarrett nodded, the humor dancing in his own gaze highlighting his resemblance to his sister. "Happens to the best of us. I'm still unclear on how she managed to rope me into the July bachelor auction, but there I was on stage." He gave a philosophical shrug. "Becca'd."

"Last year," Vicki said, "she talked me into making floats for the town Easter parade instead of going to Florida for spring break with my best friends. When they asked me why, I couldn't even really explain it. People in Cupid's Bow just don't say no to her."

"Congratulations, darlin'." Jarrett winked at Sierra. "You're one of us now."

Chapter Nine

When Jarrett finished washing up at the sink in the mudroom and entered the house Wednesday evening, he found Sierra bustling around the kitchen, her manner harried and her expression contrite.

"I know I'm the one who said it was important for you to show up for dinners," she said, "and I appreciate your punctuality. But I'm afraid I'm running late. I had a phone interview with a clinic in Fort Worth that ran long."

"No hurry." He took a seat at the table so that he was out of her way. If there was anything Sierra wanted him to do, she'd tell him. Otherwise, best not to interfere as she bounced around the room, her knee-length skirt swishing as she muttered reminders to herself.

He felt guilty about all the effort she was putting in for such paltry pay. "I appreciate you keeping Vicki fed, but you're not expected to spoil us rotten. You don't have to go all out every night. Heck, I would have been perfectly happy with leftover cobbler for dinner."

"Yeah?" She smirked over her shoulder. "Then maybe you shouldn't have finished it all at lunch."

"I regret nothing."

Her lips curved into a quick answering smile before she went back to her verbal checklist. "…sugar for the tea. Ooh, flip the fish!" She grabbed a spatula and opened the oven door. When she bent over, the silky material of her skirt lovingly hugged her butt.

Damn, the woman had a nice backside. *Which you have no business ogling.* He chivalrously shifted his gaze. Eventually.

But watching Sierra cook was a banquet of temptations. She reached above her head to grab a measuring cup from the cabinet. From the rise and fall of her breasts beneath her halter top to the smooth muscle of her calves as she stretched up on tiptoe, she was spectacular. He was fortunate enough to see breathtaking vistas every day, but the view right here was more stunning than anywhere else on the ranch.

"Vicki's watching TV in the living room," she said. "The last half of *Die Hard*, which she said is one of your favorites."

A classic. Maybe he should seize the excuse and leave before anything got harder here in the kitchen. Against his better judgment, he refused. "Now that I've sat down, it's nice to be off my feet. If you don't mind the company, I'll just stay put."

"I don't mind at all." She paused, stopping the three different things she'd been trying to do at once to smile at him. It felt like a gift. "I have to say, when I moved in, I worried about the loss of independence. I'm not used to sharing living space with anyone. But you guys make pretty good roommates. It's a lot more rewarding to cook for other people. It's really gratifying when you two compliment a meal. When I shower myself with compliments, it just feels self-aggrandizing."

He chuckled. "Even if you never lived with a significant other, haven't you ever cooked an anniversary or birthday dinner for a boyfriend?"

"Once or twice, I guess. My last serious boyfriend was a doctor, and his on-call hours were insane. Sometimes our 'dates' were watching DVRed shows together at two in the morning. Not an ideal time for a four-course meal."

She used to date a doctor. He slumped in his chair, wondering why he found that discovery so depressing. *Because it's a reminder that even if you* could *ask her out, Sierra is completely out of your league.* She was a sophisticated woman who'd gone to medical school. He was a rodeo has-been who lived with his parents.

It hadn't mattered so much when he was on the road half the time. After the Rosses' full-time ranch hand left, Jarrett and his parents agreed that it made sense for him to renovate the old bunkhouse into a place of his own. But with everything that had been happening, it was hardly the top priority.

"What about you?" Sierra asked, grating cheddar cheese into the bowl on the counter. "I've heard all about Aaron. Do you have someone special in your life?"

"No." Did he sound abrupt? He couldn't help it. His love life was the last thing he wanted to discuss. There was no version of it that wouldn't make him sound like a first-rate ass.

When the doorbell chimed unexpectedly, he took it for the reprieve it was and shot to his feet.

"Expecting anyone?" Sierra asked. "I can hold off on dinner if—"

"It's probably just one of the boarding clients stopping by to visit their horse after work. Or it could be a package delivery." Maybe one of his parents had ordered something online.

"Or someone delivering a casserole," Sierra grumbled.

That was an odd prediction. Certainly lots of friends and neighbors had brought over food and get-well cards when Vicki and his dad were in the hospital, but that had stopped weeks ago.

He crossed through the house to answer the front door and found Will Trent standing on the front porch.

"Did we make plans I forgot about?" Jarrett asked. The other night at the bar, there had been a couple of times he'd caught himself thinking about Sierra and nodding along with no real idea of what Will had just said.

Will shook his head. "Nope. I'm showing up uninvited like an ill-mannered lout. My mother would be horrified. But I brought these to make up for my rudeness." He held up a six-pack of beer. "Thought I'd come see how you were doing. If you're not too busy, we could watch a movie full of senseless violence or maybe call my brothers and play some poker. You gotta watch Jace, though. He cheats."

"Really?" That was hard to believe of a Trent.

"Nah. But telling myself that allows me to keep some dignity when the little punk takes my money."

Jarrett chuckled. "Come on in." He couldn't remember Will ever dropping by out of the blue like this. Had Jarrett really looked that grim when they'd seen each other Saturday that his friend felt compelled to check up on him? "Tell me the truth," he said, remembering how angry Denise Baker had been when she saw Will at the bar. "Did you drive all the way out here because you need sanctuary from some woman who's mad at you?"

"Pffft. Women love me," Will boasted. But then he scowled. "Except for Megan Rivers. Dang female acts like I'm—"

"Who is Megan Rivers?"

"My next-door neighbor. She moved here a couple of years ago. Probably never got on your radar because she's the mother of triplets."

Jarrett didn't get involved with single moms. He'd preferred dating women whose lives were as uncomplicated as his. *Because you're a shallow SOB.* "So Megan doesn't like you? How come?"

"Who knows? Maybe she's a hopelessly bad judge of character. Maybe her ex was named Will."

"Or Trent."

"Or maybe living with three preschoolers just makes a person really, really cranky."

That certainly seemed plausible.

"I've never seen her smile," Will said. "Ever. I tried to make her laugh once, while we were both getting our mail, and she just glared like she wanted to throw her parenting magazine at me."

"It's unlikely anyone here will pelt you with reading materials, but I can't make any guarantees. Vicki has her moody moments, and Sierra, the physical therapist, is—"

"Did I hear my name?"

Jarrett turned to see Sierra at the other end of the hall.

Next to him, Will straightened from his relaxed posture to full alert. "Hi, there. You're Sierra?" When she nodded, Will pinned Jarrett with a knowing look. "So this is why we rarely see you in town," he said under his breath. "I wouldn't leave the house, either."

"It's not like that," Jarrett hissed.

"I was hoping you'd say that." Will strode forward, offering his hand. "Will Trent. A pleasure to meet you, ma'am."

She shook his hand, glancing at the six-pack he carried. "Are you staying for dinner? I made plenty."

"My policy is never refuse an invitation from a beautiful woman."

Sierra grinned up at him and suddenly Jarrett understood exactly what it felt like to want to throw something at his friend.

For all that Sierra was coming to care about the Rosses, Will Trent's arrival was a breath of fresh air. With his jet-black hair, the man was tall, dark and handsome—although not quite as tall as Jarrett. Not quite as handsome, either. But Will's easy smiles and unrepentant flirting made him fun to be around. He didn't seem the type for any charged silences or brooding guilt. He nicknamed Vicki "Hot Wheels" and entertained her with impressions of townspeople while he lent a hand setting the table.

The only person who didn't seem thrilled to see him was Jarrett, which confused her. She knew from a couple of mentions this week that Will was the friend Jarrett had gone out with last weekend. Had she overstepped by inviting the man to stay for dinner? It had seemed like the obvious course of action. Frankly, she welcomed the silly banter he provided. Will lightened the mood.

Not everyone's.

She would have expected his buddy's presence to engage Jarrett in conversation. Instead, he seemed withdrawn, hardly saying three words as Sierra filled glasses with iced tea. He leaned against the kitchen island with his arms folded, looking more like the stoic cowboy who'd hired her than the one who'd caught her rearranging the pantry last night and teased her about being a control freak.

"Jarrett?" She called him to the corner of the kitchen, away from where Will and Vicki were joking at the table. "Can you help me get this serving bowl down?"

He nodded, wordlessly crossing the tile floor to where she waited. The scent of the soap he'd used enveloped her, pleasantly mingling with the muskier, masculine smell of him. She should move out of his way. But since she'd engineered the moment to ask privately whether it was okay that she'd invited Will to join them, she needed to be close for Jarrett to hear her whispered question. So she remained where she was and found herself wedged between the counter and Jarrett, his body pressing lightly against hers as he reached above her. Her breath hitched and he looked down, capturing her gaze with his own.

He lowered the bowl into her hands. His fingers, warm and a little rough, brushed over her knuckles, and she shivered. She barely remembered what she'd intended to ask. And she could not remember the last time she'd felt like this—palms damp, heart racing, her skin deliciously sensitive.

Get a grip, Bailey. The man handed you a bowl. He didn't undress you.

His eyes were molten silver. "Anything else I can do for you, darlin'?"

"I, um…" *Kiss me.* Not that she would ever voice such an insane request. Kissing Jarrett was completely out of the question.

Except, it didn't feel out of the question. He was watching her so intently, as if he could see her thoughts, and he was standing close enough his breath feathered over her skin. In that heartbeat, kissing him would be as natural as—

"Sierra?" Vicki's voice in the background was impatient. "We planning to eat before the food gets cold?"

Jarrett jerked away from her so abruptly she almost dropped the bowl he'd handed her. She'd missed her chance to ask him if it was all right that she'd asked Will to dinner, but, really, what would she do if he said no? Rescind the invitation and kick out the family friend?

It's too late, Bailey. Might as well go with it.

But that advice applied only to their dinner guest. *Not* her attraction to her boss.

"Well, that was an embarrassing display," Vicki said from behind her.

Sierra stiffened at the sink where she was washing dinner dishes. Now that Will had gone, was Jarrett's sister finally speaking her mind about the moment earlier when it had taken far too long for one adult to hand another one a bowl? Had Sierra's riotous feelings been visible to everyone in the room?

Battling a hot rush of mortification, Sierra turned to face her patient. Should she go with flat denial, or deem it a temporary lapse in judgment that would never happen again? But once she'd spun around, Sierra saw that Vicki hadn't even been speaking to her. She was addressing Jarrett, who'd returned from seeing Will out.

He scowled down at his sister. "I don't know what you're talking about."

"Sure you don't," Vicki scoffed. "You're thick-skulled, but you've got to have *some* self-awareness. You spent all of dinner practically snarling at one of your best friends. Honestly, Sierra's a grown woman. If she wants to go out with Will, she can."

Go out with Will? Sierra blinked. He'd told her to save him a dance at the Harvest Day Festival, but she got the impression he said that to a lot of ladies. It had been an offhand comment, not a declaration of courtship.

"Sierra's going to be here for the better part of a month," Vicki said. "Are you planning to be a butthead every time some guy comes sniffing around her?"

"Hey!" Sierra objected to the "sniffing around," which made her sound like a dog's chew toy.

Neither sibling looked her way.

"Why would I care who Sierra goes out with in her free time?" Jarrett demanded. "We've covered this before. You know I don't think of her as a woman."

"Hey!"

This time, her indignation registered. Both Rosses turned to face her, looking almost surprised by her presence.

"Do you people mind not discussing my love life like I'm not even here? Actually," she backtracked, "I'd prefer you don't discuss it at all. It's none of your damn business."

"Exactly my point," Vicki said smugly. With that parting shot, she wheeled herself from the room.

The last thing Sierra wanted was to be left alone with Jarrett after his humiliating announcement that he barely saw her as a woman. Embarrassment stung her cheeks. Had she misread that moment earlier, the way he'd looked at her? *What does it matter if you did?* She'd already vowed that she would keep her hands to herself—anything else would be foolhardy and unprofessional. Jarrett's dismissive tone made it easier to squash temptation. He'd done her a favor, really. She sure as hell didn't want to kiss him now.

What she wanted to do was storm out of the room, but the dishes weren't finished. She refused to look as if she was fleeing his presence. Sierra Bailey didn't flee. Instead, she plunged her hands into the soapy water, hoping that if she ignored Jarrett, he'd leave.

"I should apologize for my sister," he began stiffly.

"You should apologize for yourself." She scrubbed a plate with vicious force. "Not a woman?"

"Don't take it personally. All I meant is that I don't have any romantic interest in you."

She flinched at the bald rejection, not turning around as he stepped closer and grabbed the dish towel from the counter.

"And you shouldn't have any interest in me, either," he said.

"Oh, *trust* me…" She shot him a withering look over her shoulder.

Standing entirely too close for her peace of mind, he started drying the dishes she'd already washed. Damn it, he still smelled good, although she hated herself for noticing. She wanted to snap at him that she didn't need his help, but it wasn't as if she could kick the man out of his own kitchen. Nor could she break a plate over his head, but the mental image was heartening.

He took a deep breath. "I won't try to stop you if you want to date Will Trent—"

"That is so generous of you," she gushed, her eyes wide. "Letting me make my very own grown-up decisions about my own life!"

He clenched his jaw. "As the person who introduced the two of you, I feel like it's my responsibility to let you know he's just looking for a good time. Will's a decent guy, but he won't offer any kind of commitment."

"Commitment?" Did the deluded man think she was hoping to find the future Mr. Sierra Bailey during the next two and a half weeks? She slammed down a plastic cup in the drying rack. "Women aren't always hunting for husbands, you know. Sometimes, all *we* want is a good time. And, for your information, I'm not naive." Will Trent was a charmer, but he seemed like a player, the kind of guy who called every other woman "Gorgeous" because he couldn't remember her name.

Sierra had made it her entire adult life without having her heart broken. She could manage just fine without Jarrett Ross's condescending guidance.

"I never called you naive. Don't put words in my mouth! God, you're—"

"I'm what?" she pressed. It was a bad idea to bait him after he'd had the good sense to censor himself, but she was too angry to care.

Exhaling a puff of air, he stared upward as if silently praying for patience. "Stubborn. Sarcastic. Infuriating." He pinched the bridge of his nose. "But you *are* a grown woman. I'm sorry I said anything about your personal life in the first place. It won't happen again."

"Good." At least he'd admitted she was a woman. Theoretically, she'd won their argument.

But the sinking sensation in the pit of her stomach and the impotent wish she could have a do-over of the whole conversation didn't feel like victory.

"YOU SHOULD TRY these on!" The boutique owner, Jasmine Tucker, handed Sierra a pair of emerald-green slacks. "I know they're a little outlandish, but with your coloring…"

Sierra humored her, adding the slacks to the selection she had draped over her arm. "I'm not really here shopping for me," she said, more as a reminder to herself than to dissuade Jazz. The clothes were great, but since Sierra had no idea where her next paycheck was coming from after this job… "I'm just Vicki's chauffeur."

The young woman was already in a fitting room; she'd stubbornly waved away Sierra's assistance. Changing clothes in such a confined space couldn't be easy, but Sierra respected Vicki's drive to be self-sufficient.

"Well, if you find something you love," Jazz said, lowering her voice to a confidential whisper, "I've been known to give some pretty sweet discounts." She sighed. "I'm never going to break any retail profit records. I love sending people home with new outfits too much. I can't help it! I had sisters and was always stuck with hand-me-downs, so new clothes are— Ooh, this dress would look great on you, too!"

Sierra chuckled, the exchange surreal. "I can't believe I'm getting personalized fashion advice from the supermodel whose face used to look up at me from magazines in the waiting room."

"Ha! I was never anywhere close to supermodel status," Jazz demurred. "But thank you."

"Do you ever miss it?" Sierra asked. "Life in New York? Cupid's Bow must be so…quiet in comparison."

"Yes, thank heavens. There's a lot I enjoyed about New York—Broadway shows, great little restaurants with funky, unexpected menus—but my life there was exhausting. I felt like I couldn't catch my breath for four years straight. Coming home was such a relief. I know Cupid's Bow is small, but it isn't boring. The people here are much too interesting for that."

Good point. Sierra thought of some of the people she'd met—nosy octogenarian Miss Alma, Becca Johnston with her take-charge superpower, a former New York fashion model. *Jarrett Ross.* He certainly wasn't boring. Unpredictable, frustrating and moody, perhaps. But not boring.

When she'd come downstairs this morning, she'd found a bud vase with fresh-cut flowers where she normally sat at the table. Next to it was a napkin with the words *I'm sorry* scrawled across it in pen. She hadn't seen him, though, to tell him she was no longer angry about yesterday's botched exchange. How could she be? In his own misguided way, he'd genuinely been trying to look out for her, as a friend.

Maybe that's what upset you. While she recognized intellectually that it was best for them to only be platonic friends, it was somewhat ego-deflating to discover that the pull of attraction was one-sided.

"You know what?" she asked Jazz. "Maybe I will splurge on something new." Finding something that made her feel good about herself would be a nice boost.

She opened the door of a dressing room and stepped inside. A fun new purchase would be the icing on what had turned out to be a pretty great day. They'd started the day at the hospital so that Vicki could meet with her official physical therapist. Sierra had wondered if the man would resent her intrusion or question her methods, but Manuel had been thrilled to meet her. He'd invited her to take part in the session, helping to stretch Vicki's muscles and act as cheerleader when she stood from the wheelchair. She couldn't do it for long, and every single time, she broke out into a sweat almost immediately, teeth gritted as determination warred with exertion. Still, standing was a major milestone. Steps would come with time.

After PT, they'd had lunch at a quaint little deli and gone by the salon where Vicki got her hair cut into sassy new layers. Sierra had contemplated a change of style, too, but ultimately declined.

"You don't really need a new style," Vicki had said. "You're reasonably hot—for a woman pushing thirty."

"I just remembered we need to stop by the grocery store on the way home. I need to pick up some liver."

Grinning at the memory of Vicki's horrified expression, Sierra tried on a dress that was a rainbow of scarves and bandannas stitched together. Pretty. Was it casual enough for the Harvest Day Festival, or would she stick out like an overdressed thumb? She exchanged it for another outfit. The pants were so long on her they were laughable. Being petite was one of the reasons she wore so many skirts. It was difficult to find pants the right size, and she hated to bother with the hassle of hemming or custom tailoring.

When she was finished, she took the colorful scarf dress and met Vicki at the cash register. The girl looked excited about her new purchase—and showing it off for Aaron this weekend—but fatigue was beginning to shadow her face. It had been a busy day. Sierra expected her passenger to fall asleep in the car on the way back to the ranch.

But Vicki surprised her by wanting to talk. "Sierra? I'm…sorry if I made you uncomfortable last night. After Will left. I just thought it was ridiculous how my brother was acting all jealous and possessive."

Jealous? Her ego tried to cling to the word. Jarrett couldn't be jealous over her unless he was attracted to her, right?

She sternly reminded herself that attraction was a complication neither of them needed. "I don't think it was so much jealousy as protectiveness. He sees me, temporarily, as part of his household and wanted to warn me that Will is a ladies' man."

Vicki mumbled something while looking at her window. The only words Sierra caught were "pot" and "kettle."

"But as a general rule," Sierra continued, "if you want to avoid making someone uncomfortable, maybe don't speculate on her love life? If I were to go out with Will Trent or anyone else, the idea of you and

Jarrett sitting around the table and dissecting my date
is a little…"

"Invasive?"

"Ooky."

Vicki laughed. "Right. I think I remember that
word from the vocab section on my SATs. You're a
real genius, Sierra."

"Yep. That's why your family pays me the big
bucks."

SIERRA KEPT DINNER comparatively simple Thursday—
salads topped with strips of steak. If the meal turned
out to be awkward after last night's argument with
Jarrett, at least there wouldn't be many dishes to clean.
Three large salad bowls and, boom, she could escape
upstairs with a good book.

But judging from the sheepish glance he gave her
when he appeared for supper, their confrontation was
well behind them.

"Hey." He hooked his thumbs in the pockets of his
jeans. "Vicki in her room?"

"Skyping with a sorority sister about the latest
pledges chosen to join. She said to let her know when
it's time to eat."

"You, ah, saw my note this morning?"

Her lips twitched. "The napkin apology?"

A slow grin spread across his face. It was like watching sunrise. "Double-ply. When you care enough to
leave the very best."

She laughed. "For the record, I'm sorry, too. I'm
all the things you accused me of—stubborn, sarcastic. God knows my own family thinks so."

"You don't talk about them much." He pulled salad

dressings out of the refrigerator. "They're in Texas, right?"

"Houston." Which felt like a different galaxy than Cupid's Bow. "I've got three brothers, one of whom is getting married in December."

"Your parents must be so proud of you."

"Um…possibly?"

His eyebrows shot up. "How could they not be?"

"I'm sure they are, in their own domineering, 'this-isn't-the-life-we-would-have-chosen-for-you' kind of way. After three boys, Mom was really excited to have a daughter. Based on baby photos, I don't think I wore anything but pink for the first year of my life."

He eyed the vintage T-shirt she was wearing with a black skirt and boots. "I can't quite picture that."

"You'll have to take my word for it. Total pampered princess."

"What happened?"

"My fall. It made Mom and Dad see me as more fragile than ever, but it had the opposite effect on me. Once I stopped feeling sorry for myself, recovering from that injury made me realize for the first time how strong I could be. We butted heads a *lot* during my teen years." She rinsed the cutting board in the sink. "I can't imagine doing what you do—working with your family on a daily basis, living with your folks."

"I don't plan to live in this house forever." Was his tone a touch defensive? "There's a bunkhouse over the hill that I'm moving into. After some remodeling."

"I wasn't judging you," she promised. "They're lucky you're here to help with the ranch and with Vicki."

At his sister's name, his expression grew shuttered. "The luck I bring isn't always good."

In moments like these, he looked so sad. "Jarrett, I…"

He turned away from her. "I'll let Vicki know dinner's ready."

Whatever words of comfort she might have found, he obviously didn't want to hear them.

VICKI WAS IN the middle of telling Jarrett all about their day in town when she suddenly gestured with her fork, stabbing it across the table toward Sierra. "Hey, I just remembered what I wanted to ask you about on the drive home! During one of my first sessions with Manuel, he gave me some big pep talk and mentioned that it was possible for patients to ride a horse even if they couldn't walk yet. Is that true?"

Sierra choked on a bite of steak. Oh, why couldn't Vicki have asked about aquatic therapy instead? Cupid's Bow was rumored to have a spectacular community pool. Coughing, she reached for her glass of ice water. "Yes, it's true." Horseback riding aided in strengthening the leg muscles; plus, the motion mimicked the sensation of walking, helping the body relearn.

Vicki brightened. "How soon can we do that?"

"Um… That might be more up Manuel's alley than mine," Sierra admitted. "Any idea if he makes house calls? I don't… I can't really—"

"Sierra doesn't ride anymore," Jarrett said. "But Cupid's Bow is full of people who know horses. We can find someone to help get you back in the saddle, Vic. But we will need a trained therapist to supervise the process. Sierra, would you be able to manage that?" From his gentle tone, it was obvious he understood how much she dreaded being around horses.

Vicki frowned, her forehead wrinkling into lines of confusion. "What do you mean she doesn't ride 'anymore'? I feel like I'm missing something."

"I rode when I was a kid," Sierra said. "Briefly. But not since then."

"Not a problem," Vicki said. "Jarrett will teach you. Who better? He gives lessons professionally! And you guys can work on that this weekend while Aaron is here, which will give us more time alone." She nodded her head, looking pleased with herself.

Riding lessons? Something that sounded embarrassingly close to a whimper escaped Sierra. She coughed again, hoping to cover it.

"I don't think Sierra's interested in learning to ride," Jarrett said. "But—"

"Wait. Are you *scared* of horses?" Vicki asked incredulously. "That's crazy!"

"Not so crazy if you fall off one and fracture your spine," Sierra said self-consciously.

"I just meant, the idea of you being afraid of anything is crazy. I can't wrap my head around it," Vicki said. "You're…you know."

Sierra smiled, touched by the flattery. "Thank you. But everyone's scared of something."

"Uh-huh." Vicki arched an eyebrow. "So your plan is to wuss out."

"Can we go back to the part where you were implying I'm an awesome badass?"

"When was the last time you let a patient wuss out of something?" Vicki challenged.

"Um…" Sierra glanced toward the head of the table, seeking Jarrett's input. He'd been pretty supportive throughout the conversation. But now he had a hand over his mouth, clearly trying not to laugh as Vicki continued.

"Isn't the expression that if you fall off a horse, the best thing to do is get right back in the saddle?"

"Not when you break your spine!" Sierra hadn't been physically able to ride for almost a year. After that, there was no chance her parents would have risked letting their precious daughter give it another chance. By the time she was an adult, she'd long since lost any urge to try again.

"But you're all healed now," Vicki persisted. "I tell you what—if you get on a horse, I won't give you any crap for a straight week."

"Counteroffer—you don't give me any crap for a week, and I won't smother you with your own pillow."

"You really shouldn't threaten to kill me in front of a witness."

"Who, your brother? I'm not worried about him turning me in. He's easily bribed with apple cobbler."

"I'm also partial to blackberry," Jarrett chimed in.

"Come on, Sierra. Please."

Sierra tossed her hands up in exasperation. "Why are you even pushing this? I'll talk to Manuel about coming out to the ranch and working with you, so—"

"I'm pushing because it's what you would do. If there was a challenge someone didn't think they could overcome, you would harangue and nag and cajole until they succeeded."

"She's got you there," Jarrett agreed.

"Damn." She sat back in her chair, knowing that Vicki was right.

"So." He grinned at her. "What time tomorrow should I expect you for your first lesson?"

Chapter Ten

Sierra was sitting next to Vicki's mat on the living room floor, helping her rotate through foot positions as she lay on her back, when the dogs began barking wildly to signal that someone was approaching the house.

"Aaron!" Vicki's body jerked as if her first impulse was to sit straight up.

"Easy, there. Slow down so you don't cause yourself any new injuries. Let's get you into the chair. Then I can go open the door."

Vicki nodded. "You let him in, and I can freshen up. I'm sure my hair's a mess." She grimaced as they worked together to shift her position.

"Are you in pain?"

"No. Just hoping Jarrett isn't close enough to the house to accost Aaron. He'd better not be giving him the lecture about sleeping on the fold-out couch and how there will be 'dire consequences' if he's found in my bedroom."

"He's just looking out for you because he loves you."

"You have brothers, right?"

"Three."

"And did you appreciate them interfering in your love life?"

"They never tried. Probably because *I* was more likely to deck a guy for making a move than any of them were."

As much as her brothers cared about her, they favored less direct forms of confrontation. If a man seriously wronged her, Kyle would probably buy up the city block where the offender lived and have him evicted; David would look for a lawsuit angle. Michael would just report the incident to their father and let him handle it.

She'd almost got Vicki into her bedroom when the doorbell rang. Sierra hadn't given much thought to what Aaron would look like, but the blond boy on the front porch wasn't what Vicki's rhapsodizing had led her to expect. Sierra knew he was a year older than Vicki, but he was so baby-faced that it probably took him a week to develop a five o'clock shadow. He was taller than Sierra—as was the average fourth grader— but about the same height as Vicki.

"Well, hello there." He gave her an appraising look over the rims of his sunglasses. "You must be Vicki's nurse."

"Physical therapist. And you are?" It was petty of her, pretending she hadn't heard plenty of gushing about him, but the kid's smirking expression goaded her.

He scowled. "Aaron Dunn. I'm expected."

"Come on in." She opened the door wider, and he entered in a cloud of expensive body spray. "Vicki will be out in a minute. Can I get you something to drink?" She stifled the urge to offer him a snack, not wanting to sound like a suburban mom serving after-school cookies.

They went to the kitchen, making small talk about the drive. She admitted that she was still struggling to find her way around Cupid's Bow, but he was unwilling to bond over the town's lack of road signs.

Instead, he gave her a patronizing smile. "Guess not everyone's born with my innate sense of direction."

Work with me, kid. I'm trying to like you on Vicki's behalf. To be fair, if Sierra were nineteen, she might be able to see Aaron's appeal. He was cute in a generic, glossy sort of way and, to his credit, an attentive enough boyfriend that he'd driven several hours to spend the weekend with Vicki. But compared to someone like Jarrett, with his rugged appeal and slightly shaggy hair and calloused hands—

"Aaron!" Vicki entered the room, her face glowing with happiness.

He gave her a wide grin. "Every time I see you, I can't believe you're that pretty *and* so smart. The total package." To Sierra he said, "She's the only reason I passed history last semester," a confession that made her like him more.

They kissed hello, but Vicki disentangled herself before Sierra started to feel too much like a voyeur. "Sierra, I got a text from Jarrett while you were answering the door. He's ready for you down at the stable."

Sierra was 100 percent certain that Jarrett had not instigated the text exchange. Rather, Vicki had probably sent him a message that said "Horse-riding lesson! Now!" in order to get Sierra out of the house.

"Sure. Just let me get my boots."

"Which leaves you and I alone." Aaron brushed back a strand of Vicki's hair, smiling down at her. "To study history."

"Don't 'study' too hard," Sierra said. "I'll be back in a little while to make lunch." With that, she hurried out of the room before the heat of Vicki's glare burned holes in her shirt.

JARRETT SAT BALANCED atop the wooden corral fence, head tilted back so he could enjoy the sunshine on his face. It was one of those sublimely perfect days where he felt blessed not to have an office job.

At his sister's imperious text, he'd led one of the gentler horses into the fenced area and tied her lead to the railing with a quick-release knot. He'd been waiting only a minute or so when Sierra came over the small hill that separated the front yard from the acres of pasture beyond. The sun glinted off her red hair, making it even more fiery and dramatic than usual. He loved watching her move; her confidence and purpose was just shy of feminine swagger. It was impressive that she carried herself with such self-assurance even when coming to face a horse, which she'd done her best to avoid.

As their gazes met, he lifted his hand in a wave. "You look good in jeans. Very good." Where had that come from? He'd meant to say hi. "I'm, ah, used to seeing you in skirts."

Her smile was wry. "Can't ride a horse in a skirt, though, right?"

He hopped down off the fence. "I don't actually plan to put you on a horse today. I thought we'd start off slow, just basic grooming to help foster a bond. No rush."

"Right." Her eyes sparkled with humor. "I vaguely recall that you're against rushing—something about not getting good results."

She was so pretty when she smiled like that, carefree and a little bit naughty. Too bad they wouldn't be riding today—helping her into the saddle would have provided an excellent excuse to touch her. He repressed a sigh. Being noble sucked.

Yeah, well, you promised your sister. And yourself. He gestured toward the mare waiting inside the fenced area. "That's Shiloh. She's a sweetheart. I know you've had some experience with horses before, but since it's been so long, I figured we'd start with the absolute basics. You want to approach horses from the front, preferably on the left side. If the ears are back, you're not welcome. That's not usually a problem with Shiloh. Approach slowly, saying hi to her, and let her smell your hand. I don't have any treats with me, but she loves being brushed, so this whole experience will be a treat for her."

"Glad it will be fun for someone," Sierra muttered.

"You can do this."

"Damn straight. No way am I going to have Vicki heckling me all night for chickening out. So let's get this over with."

"That's the spirit." He opened the gate for her and led her inside the paddock. "Don't forget to talk to her. The calmer you are, the calmer the horse will be." Although, frankly, Shiloh's default mode was pretty mellow.

"Hey, there, Shiloh. Nice to meet you." She slowly

raised her hand for the horse to snuffle. "Please don't chomp any of my fingers off."

He tried unsuccessfully to smother a laugh.

Sierra glanced over her shoulder at him. "Have you seen her teeth? They're huge! Which figures. She's huge in general."

Seeing Sierra next to the horse was an almost comical reminder of her height. Her personality was so larger-than-life that it was easy to forget how petite she was.

A bag of grooming supplies hung over a nearby post, and Jarrett reached inside for the currycomb. "We're going to start with this to loosen dirt. You want to brush over the muscled parts of her body—stay away from the legs and face—in a circular motion."

Sierra slid her hands through the strap on the comb and, inhaling deeply, took a step closer to the horse. Jarrett stood in front of Shiloh, prepared to help calm her if necessary.

"I must seem idiotic to you," she said, "getting shaky over brushing a perfectly sweet horse who's standing still when you made a living by climbing on the backs of broncs who were actively trying to throw you."

"You know I don't think you're an idiot. Far from it." It would be so much easier to live under the same roof with Sierra if he had a more negative opinion of her. He could criticize her for being stubborn, he supposed. Or temperamental. Except that those qualities also made her determined and passionate. She might not be perfect, but she was a remarkable woman.

He turned away before he did something ill-advised—like telling her she was as extraordinary as she was beautiful. "Now we move on to the hard brush." He stepped closer to give her the brush. She smelled like cinnamon, from the French toast she'd made them for breakfast, and sunlight—sweet, warm, tantalizing.

Even though he could have talked her through the process as he had with the currycomb, he gave in to temptation and closed his fingers over hers, standing very close as he guided her hand. "Short, firm strokes," he said, demonstrating.

"Like this?"

"Yeah. That's good." Jarrett had taught dozens of people about caring for horses. Instructing Sierra should be automatic and perfunctory, not arousing.

Jarrett had always been very goal-oriented. It was one of the things that made him a winner in the ring. With past lovers, he'd focused on the act of sex itself, on making sure his partner enjoyed herself, but he'd overlooked how sexy even seemingly platonic moments could be. *Maybe because you never bothered to have platonic moments.* When a woman had demonstrated her interest in him, he hadn't spent weeks courting her before seducing her. In some ways, the relationship with Sierra was one of the most personal he'd ever had. He wasn't used to planning to-do lists with someone else, standing side by side as they did dishes, noting how adorably sleepy she looked at the end of a long day. Even arguing was new. His sexual encounters were usually amiable and conflict-free. *Shallow.*

When he'd vowed earlier this summer to change his ways, guilt had been a major motivator. Yet now he found himself craving a different kind of connection with a woman for reasons that had nothing to do with regret or mistakes. He felt as if he'd caught a glimpse of something in the distance—something rare and special and worth working toward.

"Now what?" Sierra asked.

Damned if I know. Then it registered that she was asking about equine grooming, not his sappy dating epiphany. "Uh, soft brush, to smooth the coat."

Once she was finished, he showed her how to care for the hooves, although he did it himself—partly in case Shiloh got antsy and partly to give himself something to think about other than dating. Even if he hadn't promised Vicki that nothing would happen between him and the physical therapist, Sierra was leaving Cupid's Bow in a couple of weeks. The thrill of a short-term fling with no future was exactly what the old Jarrett would have wanted.

"You did really well," he said once they were finished and Sierra was affectionately patting Shiloh's neck. "How about we follow the same routine tomorrow, and then by Sunday the two of you should be comfortable enough with each other that we can go rid—"

His words were cut off by the sound of an engine, and they both turned to see Aaron's truck roaring down the ranch's dirt road toward the main street.

"What do you suppose that's about?" Jarrett asked.

Sierra met his gaze, her expression perplexed. "We were done here anyway, right? I'll get back to the house. See you for lunch?"

"Okay." But as he led Shiloh back to her stall, he couldn't help wondering about Aaron's speedy exit. Had Vicki been in the truck with him? It was possible the two of them were going to eat lunch in town and the kid was just driving too fast to show off. But if she hadn't been with him, why was the visitor who'd just arrived leaving in such a hurry?

Knowing he wouldn't be able to concentrate on anything until he knew Vicki was okay, he tried texting her. When she still hadn't responded a few minutes later, he headed for the house. No doubt he was overreacting, but this way he could at least lend Sierra a hand with lunch.

As soon as he entered the mudroom, he heard his sister's raised voice.

"—left me for her. But who can blame him, really? *She* can walk," Vicki said, her tone thick with self-loathing. "And dance. And…do other things."

He clenched his fists. No wonder the loser had fled the Twisted R. He'd probably known Jarrett would want to pummel him.

Not bothering to remove his boots, he stomped into the kitchen, where Sierra sat next to his sister, a consoling arm around her shoulders. "I say good riddance," he growled. The sight of Vicki's puffy, tearstained face made him seriously consider a road trip to the college campus. "I'm sorry he hurt you, but that jerk never deserved you. You will find someone who—"

"Has a fetish for girls in wheelchairs?" Vicki asked hollowly.

Raw helplessness scraped at his insides. He hated seeing her in pain. "You won't be in the wheelchair forever, Vic. You'll meet other guys, better guys. You'll fall in love again, and—"

"What the hell do *you* know about love? Have you even gone out twice in a row with the same woman, or is the 'relationship' over as soon as you throw the condom away?"

"Victoria!" He sucked in a breath, staggered by the crass words and the hostility in her expression.

"Vicki, that was uncalled for." Sierra's tone was soft but rebuking. "You have every right to be upset, but Jarrett's not the bad guy. He hasn't done—"

"You have zero idea what my big brother has and has not done. The women he's slept with. The promises he's broken." Vicki's voice cracked. "M-men suck. Even the ones y-you think…you think you can c-count on."

Sierra bit her lip, looking indecisive as she glanced between brother and sister. "Maybe I should go and let the two of you talk?"

"I have nothing to say." Fresh tears spilled down Vicki's face. "I want to be alone."

"Okay." Sierra rose slowly. "Do you want any help getting back to your—"

"No. Just get out. Please." The word ended on a wail that knifed through Jarrett.

He was only distantly aware of Sierra's hand on his arm, tugging him into the living room.

"Don't worry," she whispered once they were around the corner. "I won't leave her alone for long before I check on her."

"Thanks." It would take time, but he believed Sierra would be able to help Vicki through this. In the week she'd been here—had it been only a week?—the physical therapist had earned Vicki's trust and respect. They didn't need him in the house, just another male who'd let his sister down. "I should get back to work."

"I can bring some sandwiches down to the barn later."

"Thanks, but I doubt I'll have much of an appetite."

"Jarrett." She waited for him to meet her gaze. Her green eyes shone with compassion he didn't deserve. "People in pain lash out at convenient targets. No one knows that better than physical therapists. You should hear some of the names I've been called." She squeezed his hand. "Vicki didn't mean it."

He flinched away from Sierra's touch, recalling all the lustful impulses he'd had down by the stables—the exact kinds of thoughts his sister would have expected of him. "She meant every word." He strode down the hall toward the front door. He needed to get outside, where he could breathe again. Out of this conversation, which made him feel as if he was suffocating on his own shame. "And she wasn't wrong."

Sierra followed after him, too close, crowding him. "I may not have known you very long, but—"

"Let it go. Forget about me, and focus on taking care of my sister," he said, opening the door. "That's what I pay you for."

She exhaled in an angry huff, but Sierra wasn't one to give up easily. "I'm more than just an employee. I'm your friend."

Friend? The word was so simple and benign, but it didn't begin to cover what he felt for her. "No." He stepped into bright autumn sunshine that did nothing to warm him. "You aren't."

The last thing Sierra expected to see when she opened her eyes was Jarrett's face peering down at her in the dark. She jolted upright on the couch, nearly banging their skulls together.

He moved back just in time to dodge the head

wound, and she saw he was holding a quilt. "I didn't mean to startle you," he whispered. "You looked so peaceful, I was going to cover you up and let you sleep down here."

"I must've drifted off while reading. What time is it?" she asked, smothering a yawn.

"A little after midnight." Moonlight through the window silvered his profile as he turned toward Vicki's closed door. "How is she?"

"Hard to tell. She barely said a word all night, but I curled up on the sofa with a book so I'd be close in case she needed me."

Vicki's earlier anger seemed to have drained away, leaving quiet despondency in its place. Figuring that someone who'd had her heart broken was entitled to one day of moping, she'd decided to give Vicki until morning before pressing her to talk or resume her therapy exercises. Sierra hadn't even bullied her patient into eating dinner. Although she'd cooked enough food for three people, she needn't have bothered. Shortly before seven, she'd seen Jarrett's truck drive off. He hadn't told them where he was going or when he would be back.

She arched her back, stretching. "You didn't go rough up Aaron, did you?"

"If I did, wouldn't I be pretty dumb to admit the crime to someone else?"

"Depends on how much you trust me. I could be very useful if you needed an alibi." She caught the brief gleam of his smile flash in the dimness. Earlier, she'd been reading by the light of a table lamp. He'd obviously turned it off when he'd decided to let her spend the night downstairs.

He sat in one of the armchairs, retreating into shadow. "Reckon I do trust you. Enough to tell you the truth."

"About where you were tonight?"

"Just shooting pool. I meant the truth about Vicki's accident."

Her breath stilled in her lungs, almost as if she were afraid the slightest movement would spook him and that'd change his mind. It wasn't that she wanted Jarrett to confide in her to appease some morbid curiosity; she wanted him to open up because she believed it would be good for him. Whatever misplaced guilt he felt over Vicki's accident, maybe talking about it would help him move past it. So she waited, motionless, hoping he took her silence as encouragement.

"That stuff she said this morning… About me and relationships?" His bark of laughter was full of self-deprecation. "Not that I ever experienced anything close to a real relationship. She was right about that. I liked women a lot, and I liked a lot of them."

"Not unheard of for an attractive man in his twenties," she said softly. Nonetheless, she didn't want to dwell on the thought of him with these faceless women.

"The night of Vicki's crash, she and I were supposed to go to dinner. I'd been on the rodeo circuit. She'd been away at college. We hadn't seen each other in months, and she caught a ride with a friend to come watch me compete. Then I blew her off."

She put the pieces together. "For a woman."

"I'm not even sure what her name is," he said raggedly. "I've narrowed it down to something starting with a *T*. That's how lousy a brother I am. I stood up my own sister. I sent her home in my truck so I could have a couple of naked and sweaty hours with a blonde stranger."

She tried to imagine how she'd feel if one of her brothers had done that, but she didn't have the kind of relationship with any of them that would have led to a one-on-one dinner anyway. They got together for group events as a family, but she wasn't friends with any of them. For the first time, that struck her as sad. Maybe she should take some initiative when she went home for Christmas to get to know her brothers better.

"My parents were devastated by the accident," he continued. "I'm not sure they've really recovered. Vicki was a sweet, enthusiastic kid with a bright future. You've only seen the angry Vicki who—"

"She still has a bright future," Sierra interrupted. "As you yourself pointed out today, she's not staying in the wheelchair. She's young and resilient. Her progress since I've been here has been tremendous. There's no reason she can't be back in college next semester."

"I hope she is. But I have no idea what the next few months will bring for my father. During Vicki's second surgery, he collapsed of a heart attack."

Sierra winced at the unfortunate overlap. "And you blame yourself for that, too?"

"The timing was no coincidence."

Probably not. But she suspected stress was only a trigger in conjunction with other causes. "A heart attack involves half a dozen factors, from genetics to eating habits. Shouldering sole blame for it is the height of self-absorption. The world doesn't revolve around you, cowboy." She said it lightly, but that didn't make the statement less true. "If you've made bad decisions in the past, start making better ones. But beating yourself up for other people's decisions—like the guy who chose to get behind the wheel after he'd been drinking—is a one-way ticket to crazytown."

For a moment, Jarrett didn't say anything. She hoped she hadn't sounded too cavalier about what his family had suffered, but he needed to accept that he couldn't change the past. What happened next, however, was entirely up to him. Vicki wasn't the only one who needed to move forward with her life.

"You don't think I'm a terrible person?"

"I think you're a person, period. We make mistakes." She could offer him forgiveness all day long, but it wouldn't solve the underlying problem. "Really, my opinion is irrelevant—this is between you and your sister. Have you apologized?"

"For a solid week after the accident, all I can remember saying to her is 'I'm sorry.' The words are damned inadequate, though."

"They're a start. Don't fall back on words alone. Be there for her."

"Even when she tells me to go the hell away?"

"Especially then. Obviously, there are moments she'll need her space, but too much space is just avoidance. Let her know you'll be there when she's ready to reach out." She yawned again. "Meanwhile, if *I'm* going to be there for her tomorrow, I should probably get some sleep."

"Sorry. This conversation probably should have waited until daylight hours. But honestly? It was easier to tell you in the dark."

She could understand that. But this midnight confessional had an air of intimacy that made her uneasy. On the day the Rosses had hired her, she'd told Vicki, *"I don't do 'bonding.'"* She'd said it to stem Vicki's argument that they weren't going to become friends, but, looking back, she realized the words had a lot of truth to them. She had plenty of acquaintances back in Dallas, but no one she missed enough that she'd called them during her time in Cupid's Bow. She loved her family from a distance. She was actively dodging her mom and couldn't recall an instance in her adult life when she'd sought out a brother's company just because she wanted to spend time with him. She'd slept with Paul for months, but she hadn't loved him. Was she emotionally stunted?

Nonsense. She blamed the uncharacteristic melancholy on the late hour. When she met someone worth falling in love with, she'd give it her all. Meanwhile, why settle?

She stood. "Are you coming upstairs, too?"

"Eventually." His tone was sheepish. "I thought I'd check the kitchen to see if there were any more brownies left. You're a hell of a baker."

"Nah, my family's housekeeper is a hell of a baker. I'm just an adept student. Good night, Jarrett."

"Night."

She'd made it to the bottom of the staircase when he softly called her name.

"Sierra? Just so you know, your opinion *is* relevant. What you think matters to me."

It was on the tip of her tongue to make a joke—to tell him she was glad, because she had plenty of opinions. But she couldn't do it. Instead, she climbed the steps, swallowing past a sudden lump in her throat. *You matter to me, too, cowboy.*

SIERRA WAS GROGGILY pouring her second cup of coffee when the doorbell rang on Saturday morning. Smoothing a hand over the hair she hadn't bothered to fix yet, she trudged to the front door. It wasn't until she opened it and saw Kate Sullivan standing there that she remembered they'd scheduled a breakfast meeting. They were supposed to go over all the booths and game areas with Vicki and figure out how best to use the ranch.

"Crap!"

Kate blinked. "Well, hello to you."

"I am so, so sorry." Sierra stepped out onto the porch and closed the door behind her. "It was a rough night here. Vicki's boyfriend broke up with her yesterday."

"Ouch."

"I completely forgot we were supposed to get together, and since she's still in bed, I'm assuming it slipped her mind, too."

"Understandably," Kate said, her expression sympathetic.

"I can go wake her up, but—"

"How about we reschedule? Although, it will need to be soon. The festival is almost upon us."

"Tomorrow?" Sierra said. "I swear we'll have our acts together by then. I'd volunteer for us to come to you so you don't have to make the drive again, but that kind of defeats the purpose of you getting the lay of the land here."

"Tomorrow, huh? We have a big family lunch planned

after church, but my schedule is open once that's over. And don't worry about me making the trip twice. Gram's farm isn't far. Besides, driving over here gave me a few minutes of peaceful solitude on a pretty day." She smiled. "When you're a parent, you appreciate those moments whenever you can get them."

"Thanks." She appreciated both Kate's understanding and her efforts to mitigate Sierra's chagrin. "After I have a chance to talk to Vicki, I'll text you about a time."

"Deal. But since I'm here, I wanted to ask you—are you busy tonight? Cole and I are going dancing. Want to come?"

"On your date with your fiancé? I appreciate the invitation, but I'd hate to be a third wheel."

"About that." Kate shifted her weight. "Cole's brother is planning to meet us there. Will Trent? You met him earlier in the week? When I told him you and I were working on the festival together, he mentioned he'd like to see you again."

"So this would be a double date?"

"Not at all. I just thought you might like a night out on the town before you leave Cupid's Bow. But, in the sense that I will be there with a handsome man and there will be another handsome man hoping to dance with you…" She widened her eyes, all innocence. "I can see where someone *might* think of it as a double date."

Sierra laughed. "If I ever decide I want to learn subtlety, I know who I'm coming to for lessons."

"I was once a straightforward person, but being the mother of a teenager is making me sneakier. Luke's a good kid, but he's got enough of a rebellious streak to resist the direct approach. I often have to disguise requests or make something seem like it was his idea in the first place. Not that I'm comparing you to a stubborn thirteen-year-old," she added hastily. "So, will you join us tonight?"

Sierra hesitated. On the one hand, she felt as if she should be here for Vicki. But if Vic was going to hole up in her room again, two nights in a row of couch vigil seemed lonely. *You can ask Jarrett to hang out with you.* They could play a board game or watch a movie. She thought about the two of them alone in the living room, recalling last night and the conflicted feelings that had kept her awake long after she'd crawled into bed.

"I'll go," she blurted.

"Yay! It's a date." Kate grinned. "Unofficially."

Sierra said that she wanted to take her own car, in case she was needed back at the ranch, and they agreed to meet at eight o'clock. By the time Sierra made it back to the kitchen, her coffee was cold.

Rinsing out her mug, she considered the night ahead. *I have a date with Will Trent.* Maybe not an official one—he hadn't even asked her himself—but she was spending the evening with an amusing, attractive man. So why didn't she feel more enthusiasm? Being out with him would probably be more fun than sitting around the Twisted R on a Saturday night.

It would definitely be less complicated.

Chapter Eleven

At nearly eleven, Sierra finally went in to check on Vicki, who mumbled "go away" and yanked the sheet over her face with her good hand.

"Sorry, kid." Sierra pulled the linens away. "All parties have to end eventually, and I'm declaring this pity party officially over. You'll feel better after a shower."

"I'll feel better when Aaron flunks out of history." Vicki glared. "Do you know he actually had me *edit his paper* before telling me he was seeing someone else?" She let out a shriek of fury.

"Bastard." Sierra wanted to take the anger as a good sign, but there'd been anger yesterday, too, before the despondency. "He's definitely not worth your lying in bed all day crying over him. He's a pig."

"That's an insult to pigs everywhere," Vicki said as they got her into her chair.

With the shower running, it took Sierra a moment to realize that the sound of someone knocking wasn't her imagination. "Okay," she said aloud, "there's no way I forgot *two* appointments today."

She answered the door, nearly bowled over by a trio of girls talking at once. It was hard to make out what each of them was saying, but she caught phrases here and there.

"Is Vicki okay?"

"...that rat Aaron..."

"...never be allowed to set foot in the Zeta Gamma Mu house again. Lifetime banishment!"

Sierra whistled to get their attention. "I take it you ladies are friends of Vicki's?" she asked once they were quiet. When they all opened their mouths to speak, she held up a hand. "One at a time, please."

"Not just friends," answered a curvy girl who'd cut the bottom of her sorority T-shirt into strips, creating a fringed crop top. "Sisters."

The three of them could almost pass for sisters. They were each about the same height with long, straight hair, although coloring and body shape varied.

The one in the middle wore glasses and was slender as a reed. "I'm Jemma. That's Bree and Matisse. Her mom's an art professor."

The girl in the altered T-shirt nodded. "I have brothers named Claude and Blue."

"We came as soon as we got Vicki's text," Bree said. "She sent Matisse a message last night—"

"But I'd accidentally left my phone in— Not important."

"Can we see Vicki?" Jemma asked.

"Absolutely." Sierra ushered them inside. Their company might be exactly what Vicki needed. While bad breakups sucked, venting to friends about guy troubles was such a reassuringly *normal* thing for a nineteen-year-old to do. Not like trying to reteach your legs how to support your weight or keep your pelvis perfectly aligned during standing exercises. "I'll just let her know you're here."

They trailed her down the hall, waiting as she went into Vicki's suite and knocked on the bathroom door. "Vicki? You have visitors."

The terse "who?" from the other side didn't sound very welcoming, and Sierra hoped she wasn't wrong about Vicki needing her friends right now. "Um, Jemma and—"

"My girls!" The door opened, and Vicki wheeled into the room.

High-pitched squeals and greetings ensued.

Sierra winced at the decibel. "I'll, uh, leave you guys to catch up."

Matisse beamed at her. "Don't worry. We've got it from here."

JARRETT GLANCED AT his watch. His stomach was growling and it would be nice if he had time to grab some lunch while he was in the house, but Mrs. Wilcox would be here in less than ten minutes for her boys' riding lessons. He was already pushing it by going inside to change; a morning of tractor repairs had left him covered in grease.

He banged open the door to the mudroom, already stripping off the soiled shirt to toss it in the washing machine.

The door to the kitchen opened, and Sierra hurried out to meet him. "We've been—" She stopped, her green eyes fixed on his torso with gleaming interest.

Her expression was damn good for his ego. As the moment stretched on, the urge to tease her became irresistible. "Hey," he said, "my eyes are up here."

Her face flushed with color. "I... Sorry."

Grinning, he let her off the hook. "No apology necessary. Trust me, darlin', if I ever walked in on *you* shirtless, I'd lose more than my train of thought."

The rosy hue in her cheeks deepened, and she looked away.

"What was it you were saying?" He should really find out what she needed and be on his way. Mrs. Wilcox was a stickler for punctuality. She'd once said the only way to keep five sons in line was to enroll them in so many activities that they had no time or energy left for mischief. As a result, she was always on her way to a lesson or a sporting match or to drop someone off for a part-time job.

"Oh, we've been invaded."

"Aliens? That would explain the crop circles in the pasture."

He didn't have the time to stand here making dumb jokes, but it was worth it when she laughed, her green eyes shining up at him.

"Three of Vicki's sorority sisters came to check on her," she said. "They're finishing a movie in the living room but already have plans to take over the kitchen and whip up appropriate comfort food. There was talk of something called 'armadillo eggs.' And lots of chocolate. In fact, I think I'm being sent to town with a sizable grocery list, if you need anything."

He shook his head, sidestepping her so that he could get into the house. "All I need is a clean shirt and more hours in the day." What he *wanted*, on the other hand, was to stay here with Sierra, making her laugh and enjoying the blatant interest in her gaze.

It was surprising how comfortable he was with

her after what had happened yesterday. When Vicki had attacked him about his dating habits, he'd been ashamed that Sierra was there to hear it. Yet last night, when he'd told her about his carousing and Vicki's accident, she hadn't judged him at all—except to tell him to get over himself.

His mother had also told him to stop blaming himself, but she loved him, was predisposed to believe it wasn't his fault. Sierra was blunt with her opinions. If she'd thought his actions were unforgivable, she would have said so. Instead of condemnation, there'd been only matter-of-fact advice and a willingness to listen.

For a woman who routinely branded herself "difficult," Sierra Bailey was surprisingly easy to be with.

SIERRA HAD ALREADY made one trip inside with a bag of groceries when she heard footsteps behind her. She glanced over her shoulder and saw Jarrett—wearing a shirt, mercifully. She still felt foolish over how strongly she'd reacted to the sight of him earlier. She was a medical professional, for crying out loud! She'd seen plenty of unclothed bodies.

Then again, not every man had a body like his.

"Need any help?" he called from a few yards away.

"Nah." Sunset came just a little bit earlier every day, and she knew Jarrett's weekends were the busiest because of riding lessons and the boarders who came to visit their horses. "Jemma's coming out to grab the rest of it as soon as she finds her shoes."

At Jemma's name, he darted a glance toward the house that seemed almost nervous.

"Problem?" she asked.

"Of course not." He lowered his voice, leaning toward her. "But I went inside earlier to grab a quick bite and there was so much giggling. Are you sure there are only four girls total? It seemed like more. They're trying to cheer Vicki up by making plans for the spring, like concerts by bands I've never heard of. Sierra, they made me feel almost…old."

She grinned at his horrified expression. "I had that same sensation earlier. Like I was the den mother."

"Good to know it's not just me they've prematurely aged. Maybe tonight you and I should sit side by side in rockers on the porch and puzzle over whippersnappers these days with their instatwitter and facegrams."

Speaking of tonight… She needed to tell him she wouldn't be here.

"What?" He cocked his head. "You do realize I was kidding. I know it's not called facegram."

"Hey, I made plans with Kate tonight. Is that okay? I probably should have talked to you before—"

"Of course it's okay for you to take the night off. I hired you to be with Vicki so I can put in full-time days, but no one expects you to be at our beck and call around the clock." His mouth lifted in a sardonic half smile. "Especially not for what we pay you."

She lifted one shoulder as she reached into the trunk. "You'll make it up to me with glowing recommendations to any prospective employers."

"Right. Any hot leads?"

"Yeah. That clinic in Fort Worth wants me to come for an in-person interview, but not yet. Their human resource manager will be out on vacation this coming week, so we'll schedule it after she gets back."

"Well, that's…great." His tone didn't exactly match

his words. When she shot a questioning look over her shoulder, he changed the subject. "So you and Kate have a girls' night planned?"

"Not exactly. I mean, yes. She invited me to the local dance hall, but it won't be just us. Cole and his brother will be there, too."

"You have a date with Will."

"More or less." Why did she suddenly feel guilty? "Is that a problem?"

"Why would it be?" His tight smile didn't reach his eyes. "Who you choose to spend your Saturday nights with is your business."

The front door opened, and Jemma came bounding down the porch stairs like a long-legged puppy, all youthful energy. "I promise I didn't forget about the groceries!"

I did. The last thing on Sierra's mind was the bag of food she held. She was far more concerned with trying to read Jarrett's expression, but he was already turning away.

"See you all at dinner," he said. "Assuming you'll still be here?"

She nodded. "I'm making a couple of pizzas. I'll head out after we eat."

He gave a crisp nod and headed back in the direction of the barn.

Was he angry? Disappointed that she hadn't heeded his warning about not going out with Will? The firefighter's aversion to commitment was hardly a deterrent. If Sierra's upcoming interview went well, she would be living in Fort Worth by October. The last thing she wanted was to fall for a man in Cupid's Bow.

"JARRETT? IF YOU don't grab a slice, there might not be any pizza left."

Vicki's words, which seemed to be coming from a lot farther than a few feet away, made Jarrett wonder how long he'd been standing at the counter, staring out the kitchen window. Truthfully, he wasn't very hungry. But at least his sister was voluntarily speaking to him after yesterday's blowup.

Good thing she was being civil since he'd probably alienated Sierra before she left the house. Having both the females he lived with ticked off at him seemed like a dangerous gamble.

When Sierra had come down the stairs for her date, Jarrett had been poleaxed by the sight of her in that figure-hugging black dress. He'd also noted the effort she'd put into styling her hair and fixing her makeup—trouble she'd gone to for Will Trent. He should have told her she looked beautiful. Or, better yet, said nothing at all. Instead, what he'd heard come out of his mouth was that she was overdressed for the local dance hall.

She'd narrowed her eyes. "Then maybe I'll set some new trends around here. Don't wait up for me."

Wasn't there a time when he'd been smooth with women, instinctively charming? He'd habitually doled out flattery to every female who'd crossed his path. So why, after a day of thinking how grateful he was to Sierra, had he insulted her instead of paying her a basic compliment?

Behind him, Vicki cleared her throat. "We're going to be using the TV. You didn't need the living room, right?"

In other words, could he please be somewhere else

in the house instead of awkwardly lurking around like an unwanted chaperone? "Not at all. Maybe I'll go into town."

Last night, he'd shot game after game of pool with anyone who wanted to challenge him. Tonight he could catch a movie. Or call a few of the rodeo buddies he hadn't seen much of lately and see if anyone wanted to go bowling.

But even as he had the thought, he dismissed it. Why bother lying to himself? He knew exactly where he was headed.

"YOU LOOK FANTASTIC," Kate said, raising her voice to be better heard over the live band. "I'm sure Will's already told you that."

He had, when she'd first arrived half an hour ago. Currently, Will and Cole were at the bar, getting them a round of drinks. When asked what she wanted, Sierra had said anything frozen. She normally preferred a glass of nice wine over cocktails that came with umbrellas or swizzle sticks of fruit, but two fast dances on a crowded floor had left her flushed with heat. Besides, while Cupid's Bow had a number of nice qualities, she doubted an upscale wine list was one of them.

"It's always nice to hear that you look good," Sierra said, "even if it's already been said." *Take that, Jarrett Ross.* Maybe she *was* overdressed, standing out among women who were mostly wearing jeans and red bandanna skirts, but none of her companions seemed to mind.

Lifting her hair off the nape of her neck and fanning herself with her free hand, she scanned the throng of people around her, hoping to see the Trent brothers returning with cold drinks. No such luck. "Cole seems great," she told her friend. The smiling man, who looked a lot like Will, radiated happiness every time he looked at his fiancée. "I've never met a town sheriff before. I think I expected someone more serious. All squinty-eyed and somber, ready to challenge bad guys in high-noon showdowns."

Kate's peal of laughter rang out over the band's fiddle solo. "You do know Cole's not a sheriff in the 1800s, right? Besides, it's Cupid's Bow. We're fortunate not to have too many bad guys. Mostly, our crime waves are limited to the Breelan brothers fighting among themselves and crafty old Mr. Wainwright, who has tried to sneak past the nursing-home administration to go streaking three times over the past year."

Sierra grinned. "Cupid's Bow has a senior-citizen streaker?"

"Well, he only successfully made it once. The other two times, he was spotted and cajoled back into the facility with butterscotch pudding."

"Butterscotch pudding? Y'all must be talking about Mr. Wainwright." Cole emerged from the crowd, carrying two beers. "The deputies are betting shifts of early-morning crosswalk duty on when he'll make his next attempt."

"I can't believe this," Will complained, handing Sierra a frozen margarita. "We leave you two ladies alone, presenting Kate a clear opportunity to talk me up to a beautiful redhead, and instead, my future sister-in-law decides to chat about an eighty-two-year-old." He shot a wounded expression at Kate. "Where's the love, I ask you?"

She grinned at him over the top of her beer. "Sorry. Go away again, and I'll try to do better."

"Oh, no. You've lost all credibility with me." Will dropped an arm around Sierra's shoulders. "Besides, if I keep leaving her alone, someone else is going to ask her to dance. Then where will I be? As it is, only Cole's stern cop glare is keeping other suitors at bay."

Sierra laughed out loud at that. "Stern cop glare?" She'd never met a man who looked more besotted and happy with his life than Cole Trent.

"Oh, I have one," Cole said. "But since I'm off duty tonight, I left it at home."

The four of them continued to joke around while they finished their drinks. Then Will asked if Sierra was ready to hit the dance floor again.

"Sure." She'd learned to dance years ago at her parents' country club, but she and Paul had rarely made time for it. She'd forgotten how much she enjoyed it.

They made it to the edge of the sawdust-sprinkled dance floor just in time for the last few power chords of the rollicking song. Then the music shifted into a slower ballad. Will pulled her against him—not indecently close, but definitely more snugly than he had for their previous dances.

Sierra stiffened, the contact making her feel an errant twinge of...guilt? That was ridiculous. There was no reason why she shouldn't be enjoying Will's company. They were both single adults, and he was a great dancer with a natural sense of rhythm. She took a deep breath, forcibly relaxing her muscles and leaning into him.

They matched each other's movements well enough, but there was none of the banter they'd been sharing up until now. Could Will tell she was wrestling a sense of discomfort? At the corner of the floor, he rotated their positions, and her feet collided with his.

"Sorry," he said, even though she was certain she'd been at fault. "Guess I'm not really feeling this song." After a moment, he admitted, "I got distracted."

She glanced up, surprised to see him staring intently across the room. Apparently, he wasn't just being gallant. Something—or someone—really had snagged his focus.

"Damn," he muttered under his breath.

She craned her head, trying to see what he was looking at, but her height put her at a disadvantage. "What's wrong? Bar fight? Ex?"

"I wish. At least I know how to deal with my ex." He met Sierra's gaze, his smile wry. "When you live in the same small town, you get a lot of practice running into each other—whether you want it or not. No, I spotted Amy Reynolds, this kid I've felt vaguely responsible for since her apartment caught fire. She used to date a real jerk—guy who makes the disreputable Breelans look like choirboys—but last time I talked to her, they'd broken up. Now he's with her in a dark corner. If he confronted her, I'm more than willing to ask him to back off. But if she came here with him tonight…"

She understood his dilemma. If the couple had reunited, he didn't really have the authority to make her stop seeing the guy. "Let's go find out. I'm new in town. You can tell Amy you wanted to introduce us, and we can check out the situation up close."

"Wonderful idea." He gave her a grateful smile. "My brother could use you for undercover work."

"I'd probably be terrible at it. I'm characteristically very blunt, which doesn't work well with deception. But Kate's been telling me about the merits of being sneaky."

He took her hand, but the contact felt more practical than romantic, as if he was just trying to keep from losing her in the crowd. Their progress was interrupted twice by women cooing flirtatious hellos to Will. If Sierra had been more invested in their date, she might have been jealous.

He's a great guy. There's just no spark. She'd suspected as much before she even arrived at the dance hall. She wasn't sorry she'd come—awkward slow dance aside, she was having a lot of fun—but if he asked her out again before she left town, she doubted she'd say yes. It would feel too disingenuous.

"Hey, Amy." Will's voice was deliberately cheerful, but Sierra could still see the tension he was trying to mask. Using his size, he muscled his way between her and her scowling blond companion to hug her. And, Sierra guessed, to discreetly check if she was okay.

"Will!" Amy brought one arm up to hug him, stumbling forward as she did so. "And who's this?" Even though she was holding a bottle of water and not a cocktail, her words were slurred.

"Sierra Bailey. Nice to meet you." Up close, the girl looked young, probably not even twenty-two yet. Judging by the lines on his face, the guy with her looked a few years older. Sierra definitely got a creepy vibe from him and could see why Will had been worried.

"So what are you two up to tonight?" Will said.

"We're on a date," the other man said, his tone clipped. "Which you're interrupting."

"Donavan." Amy frowned at him, blinking her glazed eyes a couple of times. "Will's my friend. Don't be rude."

"Didn't mean to be rude, baby." The man's voice turned syrupy sweet, but there was no true affection in the way he looked at her. "I guess I just like having you all to myself."

She tittered, smiling as if he'd said something romantic. "Will, you and I will have to catch up later. Nice to meet you, Sarah."

Between the volume of the music and Amy's less-than-alert state, Sierra didn't bother correcting her. Instead, she just gave the younger woman a friendly nod.

Donavan took her hand, dragging her toward the floor. "Let's dance, baby."

As they disappeared into the Saturday-night mob, Will clenched his jaw. "I hate that guy. There are rumors about him selling illegal prescription drugs. I swear he's given her something..." He stopped, shaking his head. "Sorry. I must win the worst-date-ever prize."

"No, that would go to the guy with the toe fetish who made obscene comments about my feet three minutes into our first—and last—dinner together." When he chuckled, she congratulated herself on making him smile again. He obviously had reason to worry about his friend. "Lots of people make questionable dating choices when they're young. I bet she'll wise up and kick him to the curb eventually."

Will nodded absently. "I could use another drink. You?"

"I wouldn't say no to an ice water." At the bar, they ran into a couple of the ladies she'd met at the festival-committee lunch. While she was talking with them, a fellow fireman challenged Will to a game of darts.

When Kate tapped her on the shoulder and asked, "Where's Will?" Sierra realized she hadn't seen him in a while.

"Darts, I think. We kind of split up."

Kate's mouth twisted, her eyes reflecting disappointment. "I thought you two hit it off."

"We did." Platonically, anyway. "He's a lot of fun. But…"

"But you probably aren't going to be his date to my wedding?"

"No."

"Too bad. He's been sort of aimless since his ex broke off their engagement, and you seemed perfect for him."

"I don't think he'll have trouble finding someone new," Sierra said wryly. She'd spotted him a few feet away, flanked by two brunettes.

Kate followed her gaze. "No, I suppose not. Although I can tell you for sure he's not interested in that one. She won him during a bachelor auction over the summer, and he said the resulting date was torture. She's very cloying."

That much was evident even from across the bar. Sierra watched as the woman on his left kept finding reasons to touch him. Will seemed as if he was trying to inch away, but his movements were hampered by the woman on his other side.

Sierra set her glass down. "If you'll excuse me, I'm going to rescue my date."

Will's eyes lit up when he saw her. "Sierra! Just the person I was looking for."

"You owe me a dance," she said, her tone chiding as she reached for his arm.

The brunette on his left glared but didn't try to stop them as they moved away.

"You are a very popular man," Sierra teased him.

"A mixed blessing. Why is it never the right women who try to plaster themselves all over me? If *you* wanted to make a move, for instance…" It was clear from the twinkle in his gaze that he was kidding. Mostly.

"I think Kate was hoping we would fall madly in love."

"Yeah, she has this notion that I'm still pining for the ex who broke my heart and keeps trying to help me find someone new."

"You're not pining?" Sierra asked as he led her into a fast waltz.

"No. Tasha and I met when we were both ten and dated all through high school. I loved her, and I would have married her. But when she backed out of the wedding, it occurred to me that I was single for, effectively, the first time in my life. Why not enjoy it?"

"Seems reasonable."

"What about you? Any close brushes with matrimony?"

"Not really. I was dating a doctor for a few months, until he moved out of the country. He's a great guy, but, like you, I'm not pining."

"And there's no one you have your eye on now?" he asked carefully. "The other night, at the ranch, I kind of thought…"

She abruptly stopped dancing. "Thought what?"

"Never mind. I'm probably way off base." He took her hand and twirled her, ending the conversation.

They danced through two more songs before the band slowed to another ballad. Sierra was considering excusing herself to the ladies' room when Will glanced over her head and laughed.

"Hmm," he said, "I think my competition has arrived."

"Competition?" She turned to see Jarrett hold his hand out toward her.

"Mind if I cut in?" he asked.

Unsure how to respond, she glanced back at Will.

He winked. "Maybe not so off base after all." He took a step back. "Catch up with you later?"

"All right," she agreed, suddenly a bit breathless. *From all those twirls and spins you've been doing.* Uh-huh. That was probably it.

Jarrett stepped closer, lacing his fingers with hers as his other hand slid to the small of her back.

Tiny electric sparks shot through her. It was nothing like when Will had held her. "Wh-what are you doing here?" she asked.

"Looking for you. There's something I forgot to tell you earlier."

They were swaying together, her feet moving in time with his, but the music faded into the background when he spoke to her. All her senses were focused on him—the way he smelled, the heat of his body against hers, the silvery gleam in his eyes. He bent close, his voice a murmur in her ear. "You look incredible tonight."

Her breath caught. *That* was what he'd wanted to say? "You drove all the way into town to tell me I look incredible?" Her brain was having a tough time catching up. "You said I was overdressed."

"That's because I'm an ass. A jealous one, apparently."

"Jealous over Will? He and I aren't even interested in each other romantically." Had everyone mentally paired them off as a couple?

"I still envied the time he was spending with you. You've been dancing with him. He got to hold you, laugh with you. *Be* with you. I only have a couple of weeks left with you, darlin', and I find myself irrationally resentful of the moments we don't spend together."

She felt faint. *That's what you get for not remembering to breathe.* She'd been too spellbound by his unexpected declaration for anything as mundane as inhaling and exhaling. "I think…I think I need some fresh air."

They abandoned the floor midsong, and she made a beeline toward the exit. Outside, the night was cool against her skin, but the second she looked into Jarrett's eyes, she was feverish again.

He spoke first. "I hope I didn't upset you with what I said."

"No." Agitated, maybe, with the way her heart was slamming against her ribs and her mind was racing, trying to find the right response to his words. But she wasn't upset. "I'm glad you showed up here. Glad I got to dance with you."

"We don't have to stop," he said, pulling her closer. The music was muffled but still audible from the parking lot.

"But maybe we should." Despite her sensible words, she leaned into him, indulging herself in the feel of their bodies tangled together. Her hands glided up his back. This was such a bad idea. "I work for you. Do you know why I left my last job? Accusations of fraternization with a male patient. My professionalism is very important to me." She was beginning to realize her job was all she had. "I would never compromise myself with a patient."

He brushed his thumb over the corner of her mouth, and she shivered. "Then I guess," he said as he lowered his head, "it's a good thing I'm not your patient."

Chapter Twelve

Jarrett hadn't known what to expect when he'd parked his truck outside the dance hall. He wasn't sure he'd be welcome, although he'd hoped Sierra would be happy to see him once he'd apologized. Never in his wildest imaginings could he have predicted that minutes after finding her, they'd be kissing in the moonlight.

Even as his lips captured hers, part of him couldn't believe it was happening. She was hot and sweet in his arms, lifting on tiptoe to meet him. He threaded his fingers through her hair, determined to make this stolen moment worth it. Instead of rushing, devouring her after wanting her for days on end, he traced the seam of her lips with his tongue, coaxing, seducing. He nipped at her full lower lip and drank in her soft moan as if it were exquisitely aged bourbon. It went straight to his head.

Their kiss grew hungrier, and his need for her sharpened. He desperately wanted to touch her, but Sierra deserved better than being groped in a parking lot.

He dropped his hands to his sides, breathing heavily. She pressed her fingers to her lips, looking dazed.

"For the record," he said hoarsely, "that didn't lessen

my opinion of your professionalism one iota. You're a fantastic physical therapist. Nothing that happens between us alters that." Their kiss was about the chemistry between them and how the more he got to know Sierra, the more he wanted her. It had no bearing on the job she was doing with Vicki.

Vicki. His stomach knotted as he thought about the assurances he'd made that he'd stay away from Sierra, that he wasn't lusting after her. For now, he shoved away the recriminations. He couldn't bring himself to regret what had just happened.

And he prayed Sierra didn't regret it, either. She still hadn't said anything.

"You're quiet," he said, tucking a strand of hair behind her ear. "It's disconcerting."

"Good." Her mouth curved in an impish half smile. "I like to keep you on your toes."

If he were any more "on his toes" over her, some ballet company was going to draft him. "Do you want to go back inside?"

"I don't think so," she said slowly.

He nuzzled her neck, dotting a line of quick kisses toward the strap of her dress. "Any chance you want to make out in my truck?" he teased.

She huffed out a soft sound that was half sigh, half chuckle. "That's probably not a good idea."

Which didn't mean she didn't *want* to, he noted happily.

"I have a lot to mull over, and a raucous dance hall on a Saturday night doesn't seem conducive to deep thought."

"Do you want me to drive you back to the ranch?

We can get your car tomorrow. Or I can follow you," he offered, trying to give her the space she needed.

"That sounds good. But I shouldn't leave without letting Kate and Will know." She pulled her cell phone from the pocket of her dress and sent a text. The response was almost instantaneous. "Okay."

He reached for her hand. Even though the walk to her car was only a minute or two, he wanted the contact between them. Once she'd unlocked her door and slid inside, he bent down to press a kiss to her forehead.

"Don't think too hard," he said lightly.

She cupped the nape of his neck and pulled him down for a proper kiss. "No chance of that," she said once she'd released him. "I don't think I've been in my right mind since I got here."

Sierra woke up to the blessed aroma of coffee wafting up the stairs and serious doubts about kissing her employer the night before.

When she and Jarrett had pulled up to the ranch, Vicki and her friends had been out on the front porch, enjoying the cool breeze as they chatted. Vicki had wanted to hear about her "date," although Sierra insisted she and Will were nothing more than friends. She'd evaded questions about the evening but let the girls talk her into having a late-night ice-cream sundae with them. There hadn't been any real privacy with Jarrett to discuss the kiss they'd shared.

Maybe that was for the best, since she still wasn't sure what to say.

You could say "kiss me again, cowboy." A great plan, except that the kisses would only make her crave more. *Too late.* She'd ached throughout the night thinking about his mouth on hers. For the first time since she'd come to the ranch, she'd been too hot to sleep. And she knew the air conditioner wasn't to blame.

Her jumbled sheets were a testament to the restless night she'd spent. Sitting up, she swung her feet to the floor. *Coffee.* At this point, it was her only hope of coherence.

She was accustomed to having the kitchen to herself in the mornings, since Vicki was often still in her room and Jarrett was usually outside working at an early hour. But today, everyone was piled into the sunny room. Vicki's sorority sisters were leaving sometime after breakfast, and all four girls were seated at the table, bemoaning their imminent separation. Meanwhile, Jarrett leaned against the counter, drinking his mug of coffee.

Sierra's hand flew to her tousled hair. In her polka-dot sleepshirt and the cut-off sweatpants that served as pajama bottoms, she was a far cry from the carefully made up and accessorized woman who'd left the house yesterday evening. She wasn't indecent in her sleepwear, but she also wasn't polished. That only came after caffeine.

Yet as soon as Jarrett saw her, a slow, admiring smile spread across his face. His gaze swept over her from head to toe, the desire in his expression so evident that she almost blushed, glad none of the coeds happened to be looking his way. Despite the uncertainty plaguing her this morning, she had to grin back at him. There should be a special place in heaven for men who could make a woman feel this beautiful when she first rolled out of bed.

She went straight to him. "I'm surprised to find you here."

"I was waiting for you," he said. "I thought, since Vicki's going to want to spend a couple of hours with her friends before they leave, maybe you'd be free for your next horse-riding lesson."

Strategically, now might be the perfect time for her to get back in the saddle; she'd probably be too nervous about what was happening between her and Jarrett to remember to be scared of the horse.

He covered her hand with his. "Please?"

She melted inside, unable to resist the combination of his earnest tone and beguiling expression. He'd told her last night he wanted to spend as much time with her as possible during her remaining days in Cupid's Bow. *Admit it—he's not the only one who feels that way.*

"Okay," she agreed. "How about I meet you at the stable after I've had sufficient coffee and changed my clothes?"

"See you soon." He winked at her and headed for the door.

Oh, Sierra, what are you doing? Sighing into her coffee over a handsome cowboy didn't seem like the most professional way to spend her morning. Then again, as he'd pointed out, *he* wasn't her patient, so was there any real conflict?

"Hey, Vicki, do you need me for anything right now? I was, um, planning to meet your brother at the stable. F-for my next riding lesson." She stammered through the explanation, but luckily, Vicki would attribute that to her fear of horses.

"Go for it!"

Well, that was one option.

After a very small breakfast, Sierra pulled on a pair of jeans and a short-sleeved silky top. The shirt wasn't standard-issue Western wear, but it was fitted enough not to flutter around and spook her horse without restricting any of Sierra's movements. Similarly, her cute fall boots hadn't been purchased for tromping around a barn, but the heel was appropriate for riding. She braided her hair and applied lip gloss as a quick concession to vanity. Meeting her own gaze in the mirror, she wondered if Jarrett would discover for himself that the gloss was chocolate-flavored. A rush of anticipation went through her.

Jarrett was waiting for her at the practice ring, his elbow propped on the fence behind him. With his black cowboy hat shading his handsome face, he was the Texas rewrite of Prince Charming.

"Sorry if I took longer than expected," she said.

He tipped back his hat with his index finger, smiling into her eyes. "You were worth the wait. Are you ready for this?"

No. But that didn't seem to be stopping her.

Shiloh was saddled and standing in the corral. Another horse was saddled and tethered to a hitching post on the far side of the paddock. As she had last time, Sierra approached the mare from the left, speaking softly.

Jarrett nodded approvingly. "I'm going to help you mount and lead you around the ring once just so you can get a feel for being on her. Then I'll turn the reins over to you and go through some basic skills—stops, starts, turns."

He stepped closer, only a breath between his body

and hers, and her pulse kicked up a notch at his nearness. "Hold these like this," he said, sliding the leather reins into her hand. "I'll boost you up on three so you can put your foot in the stirrup. Swing your leg over and grab on to the pommel."

"Got it."

He hooked two fingers into the D ring on the saddle strap, his free hand moving down the back of Sierra's thigh until he'd reached behind her knee. "One, two, *three*."

Here goes nothing. Taking a deep breath, she did as he'd instructed. Between the two of them, she achieved enough momentum to land correctly in the saddle. Shiloh shifted beneath her, adjusting to the weight, and apprehension roiled in Sierra's stomach. The deal with Vicki had been that she'd get back in the saddle, right? *Achievement unlocked.* Maybe she could get down now.

Jarrett chuckled. "You should see your face."

"Sheet-white and terrified?"

"Equal parts reluctant and resolute. You look like you're at war with yourself. Also, you should probably never play poker. You'd be a complete failure at bluffing."

She arched an eyebrow. "I'm not a complete failure at *anything*," she said haughtily.

"Ah, there's the boldly self-assured Sierra I was looking for." He took the reins from her and patted Shiloh's neck, telling her what a good job she was doing. Sierra suspected the words were for her benefit as well as the horse's.

Jarrett started them off at a pace so slow it barely

qualified as a walk, but steadily increased his speed every few feet. "How are you doing?"

"I feel very tall up here." Her undisciplined gaze dropped to the back of his jeans. "The view's nice."

When he cast a quick glance back at her, she lifted one hand from the pommel to indicate the pasture beyond and the horizon that seemed to stretch on forever.

He smirked. "Uh-huh. Well, if you're done enjoying the view, I think you're ready to proceed to the next step." He gave her a brief refresher on using the reins and directing the horse, and then she was on her own.

She felt like a kid riding a bike for the first time without training wheels—exhilarated and scared and triumphant. On her second pass across the corral, she leaned forward and tapped Shiloh with her heels, urging the mare to pick up her pace. They moved on to a trot, and Sierra regretted the years she'd let pass before getting on a horse again.

"You look like you're having fun," Jarrett observed. "Up for a short ride?"

"Definitely."

He grinned proudly. "I was hoping you'd say that." He untied the other horse, explaining that Major was the lead horse on trail rides. "Shiloh's used to following and won't give you any trouble."

His assurance proved true. The path was obviously a familiar one to Shiloh, and she stuck to it complacently, although she seemed to enjoy letting loose in the open section where Jarrett said it would be okay to try a canter. Racing across the meadow left Sierra's heart in her throat, but in a good way, like screaming down a roller coaster with a best friend. Still, she knew she wasn't up for a gallop yet and she doubted she'd ever try to jump a horse again, even with a helmet.

It was enough to know that she'd accomplished this and could enjoy riding with Jarrett from time to time. *You have no time. You'll be gone soon, remember?*

All the more reason to make the most of the moments they did share.

As they returned to the corral, she gloried in a giddy sense of freedom, knowing she was no longer constrained by old fears and wounds. She felt wonderful, although there was a slight tenderness along her inner thighs. The ride hadn't been long enough for her to get sore, but she was definitely more aware of parts of her body she didn't always notice. That awareness only heightened when Jarrett helped her down from the horse.

His hands settled on her hips, his gaze dropping to her face, and the twinges she'd felt between her legs escalated to a far more substantial ache. She met his eyes, not even trying to hide how much she wanted him.

He sucked in a breath. "Have I mentioned how grateful I am that you don't have a poker face?"

Leaving the horses temporarily secured in the paddock, he tugged Sierra into the stable. They'd barely made it through the wide entryway before he spun her against the wall and claimed her mouth in a ravenous kiss. His tongue dueled with hers, and he sucked hard at her bottom lip. Need shot through her. She gripped his shirt in both hands, never wanting to let him go.

She tilted her head back against the wooden beam as he kissed his way to the hollow of her throat. He caught the hem of her satiny shirt between his fingers. "Soft." Then his hand skimmed beneath the material over her skin. "Softer."

There was a fleeting ticklish sensation as his fingers grazed her ribs, but then he palmed a breast through her bra, and the would-be giggle she'd suppressed turned into a moan. When she tried to reach up on her toes to kiss him again, she almost lost her balance. No surprise, since she'd been unsteady since the second she'd slid down from the saddle and into his waiting arms.

"Blasted height difference," she muttered. "I'm too short."

"What you are is perfect." He scooped her up and carried her to the back of the stable, setting her on her feet long enough to pull a folded picnic blanket from a cabinet. He opened it with a flourish, dropping it on the ground and then pulling her down with him. He kissed with intent, every stroke of his tongue against hers making her a little bit crazier with desire.

Both his hands were beneath her shirt, and she was about to sit up and remove it completely when the horse in the nearest stall neighed, jolting her from her sensual reverie.

"Wait." She pressed a palm against Jarrett's chest, trying to focus on regaining her composure and not on the hard, unyielding muscles beneath her hand. "No, I—"

"No?" He scrambled back, looking crestfallen.

"Well, yes." Definitely yes. "But not now." She needed to get back to the house before Vicki's friends left, needed to make lunch and be ready for their meeting with Kate. No way would she flake out on her friend two days in a row. "And not here." Good Lord—was there hay in her hair? She really was living the cliché.

He nodded in immediate agreement, but he was clenching his jaw, betraying the effort it took to move away from her. "Later, then?"

Her heart beat triple time. "Later." The word had never sounded so sexy.

The timing worked out perfectly—Sierra and Vicki had finished lunch and a set of PT exercises when the doorbell rang.

"Come on in," Sierra said, ushering her friend inside. "Sorry I didn't have the chance to tell you goodbye properly last night."

Kate waved off the apology. "It would have taken us fifteen minutes to find each other in the crowd to exchange a two-minute farewell. Texting was quicker. I'm just glad I had my phone out to show Anita pictures of the flower-girl dresses I found for the twins, or it would have taken me longer to notice." She laughed, patting the large binder in her hand. "Right now, I feel like my life revolves around two binders— wedding stuff and festival plans. Thank goodness the Harvest Day event is, as the name indicates, a single day. The Watermelon Festival back in July was four."

Sierra blinked. "How many festivals do you people have?"

"It's a small town," she said fondly. "We have to make our own entertainment."

They'd discovered last night that they had each lived in Houston. After her husband's death a couple of years ago, Kate had deliberately sought out the slower pace of small-town life. While she admitted that Cupid's Bow could be a little quirky, she embraced its eccentricities. Sierra was undecided. She missed the convenience of take-out Thai food, but she was growing accustomed to sleeping with only the sounds of nature outside her window and not city noise. And there was no question that she'd rather hang out with Kate and the Trent brothers and Anita Drake than the surgeons and attorneys she'd met at her parents' country club.

Cupid's Bow had its charms. Her gaze went to the huge bay window and the barn in the distance. She couldn't see Jarrett from here, but knowing he was out there somewhere made her smile.

Kate cleared her throat delicately. "Penny for your thoughts?" She glanced outside as if trying to find what Sierra was grinning at.

"I'm just having a good day."

They convened in the kitchen, where Kate spread out a bunch of papers on the table. The yellow sheets of paper had specifically scheduled events like games, performances and competitions. Typed on white pages were the names of different vendor sponsors who were helping pay for the festival and would each get a booth in return.

"We definitely have room for all of this," Vicki said, studying the list she'd compiled while Kate talked. "The biggest challenge will be parking. Can I make a suggestion?"

"Please." Kate nodded emphatically. "This is my first major volunteer project for the town. If I screw it up, my husband might not get reelected as sheriff."

Vicki laughed. "Sierra said that you originally volunteered your grandmother's farm, which is close by.

It's not big enough for the festival, but do you think we can use it for the majority of guest parking? We can set up a rotation of volunteers to bring people from the farm down to our ranch via hayride."

"Sounds great," Kate said. "I'll run it by Gram, but I can't imagine her saying no."

"Good." Vicki propped her chin on her fist. "As long as we have places for people to park and a place for the portable potty trailers to set up, I think everything else will run smoothly."

They discussed the different areas of the ranch and how best to divide them. Sierra was impressed with Vicki's ideas, but the longer they talked, the more she worried that Vicki wasn't being very realistic about how much she could actually oversee on the day of the festival. The uneven outdoor terrain was not ideal for her wheelchair. She wouldn't be dashing from one tent to another.

When she tried to gently remind Vicki of that, the girl scowled. "I'm getting better at the standing exercises, and I took steps on Friday morning." With Sierra's assistance, she'd been practicing to show Aaron when he arrived. He'd left before a demonstration could take place. "The festival's not until next weekend. Maybe if I work hard, I can use a walker to—"

"Vicki, I applaud the ambition, but there's a huge difference between half a dozen steps in a controlled environment and being on your feet all day." The ground that was imperfect for the wheelchair would be downright dangerous with a walker. It might be months before Vicki was ready for hills, rocks and gopher holes. "I'm not saying you have to stay confined in the house—we'll get you set up at a volunteer table or the booth of your choosing—but you'll need to delegate some of the plans you've brainstormed."

"I have lots of willing bodies on the committee," Kate said quickly. "But we need you to point us in the right direction."

Vicki wavered, and Sierra could see her weigh the heady responsibility of being in charge against the frustration of her limited mobility. She smiled tightly. "Well, I suppose the festival *is* a team effort."

They worked for another half hour or so, with Kate and Vicki splitting up a number of phone calls that needed to be made this week.

"Give me the tough requests," Vicki said, "the ones people are most likely to refuse." She tilted her head, making her eyes huge and pitiful. "Who's going to say no to the kid in a wheelchair?"

Kate laughed. "Nice dealing with a kindred devious spirit." She packed all the loose sheets of paper back into her binder. "Now I'd better get home and figure out how I'm going to trick the twins into eating lima beans for dinner. Oh, speaking of food! Sierra, can you walk me out? Gram sent some of her famous jalapeño peach preserves, but I forgot to bring in the jars."

"Sure thing."

As the two women descended the porch steps, Sierra thanked Kate again for coming back and for including Vicki in the decision-making process.

"Hey, today benefited me as much as her. I wasn't expecting Becca to give me nearly so much power, but she's preoccupied with upgrading her house so that she can rent out a couple of rooms. I don't want to screw up the festival, and Vicki had some really great input." She opened her car door and leaned inside, grabbing an oblong box with three jars of preserves bearing homemade labels. "The whole Ross family is great, don't you think?"

"Well, I haven't met the elder Rosses, but Vicki and Jarrett—"

"I was sorry I didn't get a chance to say hi to him last night. Will said the two of you disappeared immediately after your slow dance." She nudged Sierra with her shoulder. "Guess that means the two of you were anxious to be alone?"

Too late, Sierra realized she'd been asked outside so that her friend could interrogate her about Jarrett. *Ambushed by the old peach-jam-in-the-car scam.* When was she going to remember that no matter how sweet Kate was, she was also sneaky?

She rolled her eyes, carefully not meeting the other woman's gaze. "Oh, for pity's sake. Last night, you were trying to play matchmaker between me and Will, and now, less than twenty-four hours later, you've imagined some grand affair between me and Jarrett? Have you ever considered that you're suffering from wedding brain? You and Cole are so deliriously happy, you're hallucinating potential romances all around you."

"Nice try. But Will doesn't have 'wedding brain' and he sees the chemistry between you and Jarrett, too. After Jarrett unexpectedly showed up last night, Will said that, with the sparks between you two, he never stood a chance. Not that he sounded upset, so don't let that make you feel guilty."

Part of Sierra was dying to tell someone about the kiss he'd shocked her with last night, if not the more intimate details of their make-out session in the barn. But it was still so new. She'd barely had a chance to process it herself, much less figure out how to explain it to someone else. What if Kate asked about the future? Right now, Sierra's future was no more than a couple of touchstones in the murky distance—her interview in Fort Worth next week, her brother's wedding in a couple of months. She hadn't planned for a sexy cowboy with silvery eyes and decadent kisses.

"Uh-oh." Kate misread the long silence. "I ticked you off with my prying, didn't I? I don't mean to meddle but— Well, I do, actually. It's the Cupid's Bow way. But I genuinely care about you."

Sierra impulsively hugged her. "Thank you. In a town this size, it would be easy to feel like the outsider, but you've made me feel like I belonged since the day I got here."

"So you'll forgive me for all the intrusive questions about your love life?"

"There's nothing to forgive. You're just being a friend."

"Exactly." Kate ducked into the driver's seat. "Are you *sure* there's nothing between you and Jarrett?"

"Kate!" If her friend didn't drive away soon, Sierra would end up spilling everything.

"All right, all right. I can take a hint." She closed the door, giving Sierra one last cheery wave through the window.

As she watched Kate drive away, Sierra gave in to the impulse to say the truth out loud, if only to herself. "There is definitely something between me and Jarrett." But only time would tell how deep it ran.

JARRETT STAYED AWAY from the house past sundown, stalling because he was half afraid he'd pounce on Sierra the second he saw her again. He'd been hard for her all afternoon, ever since she'd met his eyes with that sultry gaze and murmured, "Later." That promise had been taunting him for hours.

When he finally walked into the kitchen, he was met by the enticing smell of dinner, but he barely tasted the roast beef she served. Instead he kept remembering the night she'd brought him a roast beef sandwich and accused him of avoiding her. Maybe he had been, at first. But noble intentions and distance hadn't done him any good. She'd got under his skin all the same. Now, instead of taking sensible refuge in the stable, he was tracking her down in dance halls just to tell her she looked nice. It was almost hilarious.

There were only two things that kept him from appreciating the humor in the situation. First, she was moving away. Driving into town to find her was one thing; routinely driving to Fort Worth was out of the question—especially when he'd need to be here to make sure his father didn't try to take back too much of the workload. Second, as much as he wanted Sierra, as impatiently as he was awaiting bedtime tonight, he couldn't entirely escape the guilt over betraying his promise to Vicki.

Falling into bed with Sierra was exactly what his sister had predicted when he'd hired the beautiful redhead, exactly what he'd sworn wouldn't happen.

You haven't done it yet, his conscience pointed out. *There's still time to change your—*

Like hell. He was losing Sierra soon—he couldn't change that—but knowing that their desire was mutual, that he'd somehow won over this fiery woman, there was no way he would sacrifice this chance to be with her. He'd sworn to Vicki that attraction to Sierra had nothing to do with offering her the job, and that was still true. Making love to Sierra didn't retroactively taint his decision to hire her. She'd absolutely been the right person for the job, which she'd proved time and again.

"Jarrett?" Across the table, Sierra looked concerned, and he realized how withdrawn he'd been. Trying to keep his simmering lust under control had prevented him from interacting much with her. He hadn't said much to Vicki either, but she was quiet, too, probably missing her friends.

"Anything wrong with your food?" Sierra asked.

"Sorry. Guess my mind's…elsewhere." Specifically, upstairs. In a bed with her. But he took a couple of bites of dinner, not wanting her cooking to go to waste.

A few minutes later, Vicki gave up on her own meal and announced that she was going to bed early. After she left the room, Sierra stood.

"The good news is, we have plenty left over for lunch tomorrow." She carried her plate and Vicki's to the sink.

"I'll clean up the dishes," he volunteered.

"You sure? That would be great. I was thinking about taking a bubble bath. I could use the relaxation. I've been…strangely tense all day."

"Go take your bath," he said softly. "If that doesn't relieve your tension, we'll see if we can come up with something more effective."

She grinned, her eyes shimmering with banked heat. "Good to know I have options."

She went upstairs and he cleaned the kitchen, then

watched some football. But it was all kind of a water-color blur, pale and muted compared to the moments he spent with Sierra. Wanting to give her plenty of time, he considered calling his parents; he'd been giving them updates on the ranch and Vicki's progress every few days. But he opted against it, afraid his mom might take his distraction as a sign that something was wrong.

He headed up the stairs, struck by the novelty of how rare it was to be with a woman under his own roof. There'd been a few furtive encounters at the ranch over the years, but a lot of his love life had taken place in motel rooms and the bench seats of trucks. When was the last time he'd woken up next to a woman he'd fallen asleep beside and started the day with her? He'd seen quite a few lovers naked, but he was woefully inexperienced when it came to actual intimacy. He liked that he knew exactly how Sierra fixed her morning coffee and how adorably disheveled she looked in her polka-dot pajamas.

He went into the bathroom for a quick shower, and the perfume of honeysuckle-scented bubble bath lingered in the air. He found the fragrance deeply arousing because now he knew what her skin would smell like when he slid into her. After his shower, he pulled on a pair of drawstring pajama pants but didn't bother with a shirt or boxer briefs. He wanted as little between him and Sierra as possible.

He brushed his teeth, getting ready for bed just like he did every night. But this wasn't any other night, and his fingers trembled as he replaced the cap on the toothpaste. The walk down the hallway was unnaturally long. He raised his fist to rap against the door with his knuckles, but it wasn't closed all the way and swung open as soon as he made contact.

She was sitting on the edge of the bed, wearing a button-down emerald sleepshirt with a satin collar and cuffs, a feminine play on a man's dress shirt.

"What, no polka dots?" he teased as he closed the door behind him.

Her smile was uncharacteristically shy. "This was the best I could do. I didn't exactly pack sexy negligees with me for this trip."

"You don't need fancy lingerie to be sexy." He walked to her and took her hands in his. "You already look like a fantasy come to life."

Her grin tipped up, more confident and sultry. "Had a lot of fantasies about me, have you?"

"Maybe one or two." Or a hundred.

"What's your favorite?" she asked.

He sat next to her, running his fingers through the damp silk of her hair. "The one where you say 'make love to me.' I'm not a complicated man."

She fell back on the mattress, pulling him with her. "Make love to me, cowboy."

"Yes, ma'am."

Chapter Thirteen

Sierra's life centered around physical responses and understanding the human body. But even with her vast knowledge, she was amazed by the overwhelming kaleidoscope of sensations she felt at Jarrett's touch. The weight of him over her, the stroke of his fingers along her upper thigh, the playful sting as he gently bit her earlobe—it was all jumbled together in a dizzying, addictive heat.

His mouth brushed over hers in teasing, minty kisses that made her desperate for more. Not a woman to be passive about what she wanted, she cupped his face and kissed him deeply. She felt his groan throughout her body, a rumble of approving thunder. By the time he unbuttoned her shirt, their kisses were becoming frantic.

He traced the slope of her breast with his lips. "I think you're my new favorite dessert," he said, glancing up with wicked eyes before his tongue flicked across her nipple.

She arched beneath him as he enthusiastically devoured her. Her hips rose to meet his in an unconscious rhythm that grew faster and more abandoned. Pleasure tightened inside her, and she trailed her fingers down his rock-hard abs until she slipped past the waistband of his pants and found something even harder.

He drew in a sharp breath, thrusting against her hand. "Damn, that feels good."

"You'll feel even better inside me," she said, barely recognizing the husky, passion-drugged voice as her own.

"I didn't want to rush you." He brushed his fingers over the excruciatingly sensitive skin of her inner thigh, closer and closer to where she needed him. "I wanted to make sure you—"

She grabbed his hand, shutting her eyes and breathing hard, not wanting to spiral any closer to the edge without him. "Trust me. I'm—" she parroted back his words from the ring earlier today "—'ready to proceed to the next step.'"

He grinned against her skin. "Smart-ass." Moving away from her just long enough to strip off his pants, he retrieved a condom from the pocket. She'd never been so happy to see a foil square in her entire life. He tore open the wrapper and she watched with unabashed eagerness as he unrolled the latex over the length of his erection.

He braced himself over her, and just as she was thinking the intensely possessive look in his eyes was the sexiest thing she'd ever experienced, he pushed inside her. After that, there was no thinking at all. He was big, but she was so ready for him that there was no discomfort, only tantalizing friction as she tightened around him.

Lacing his fingers through hers, he held her hands against the mattress as he moved inside her. He kissed her and the tight spirals of pleasure she'd experienced earlier were back, coiling and twisting and building on themselves until she shattered with an involuntary cry of release. Jarrett gripped her hips, thrusting into her more fervently, then following her over the edge. He buried his face in the crook of her neck and squeezed her to him. Squashed under his six-foot-plus frame, panting for breath and sweaty, she was utterly, blissfully content.

Would *wow* be a completely unsophisticated thing to say right now?

Eventually, he rolled off her, flopping onto his back but still holding her hand. Dazed, she watched the ceiling fan whir above them. It was set to a high speed, but hopelessly outmatched by the heat they'd just generated.

Thinking about the sky she couldn't see beyond the ceiling, she chuckled. "I've been meaning all week to go out one night and do some stargazing. I wasn't expecting to see stars in my own bedroom."

He propped himself up on his elbow, smiling down at her. "There were stars?"

"Shooting stars. Supernovas. A majestic orchestral score. It was like the best astronomy documentary ever."

He laughed. "For the sake of my fragile male ego, I'm going to pretend you didn't just compare me to a film in science class." After a moment, he said, "We'll go stargazing before you leave. You, me, a picnic blanket in a secluded corner of the pasture…"

Before she left. She swallowed, not wanting to think about that right now. "Do you know the names of a bunch of constellations?"

"Beyond the Big Dipper, no. But I'll learn them all if it impresses you."

She grinned at the idea of his still working to impress her even after he already had her naked.

For a few minutes, they lay there in companionable silence. Her eyes were starting to drift closed when he admitted, "I'm starving."

She wasn't surprised. Neither of them had eaten much at dinner. Had he, like her, been too keyed up with anticipation? "I wonder if we'd disturb Vicki if we went down to the kitchen for a late-night dessert run."

"Hey." He rubbed his thumb over her hand, his voice suddenly serious. "About Vicki… I think it would be best for her if she doesn't know there's anything between you and me."

"Huh." She bit her lip, considering. As he'd noted this afternoon, she had no real poker face. Being deceptive did not come easily to her. If she couldn't keep Will Trent and Kate from seeing her attraction to Jarrett, how long would she be able to hide it from someone who was living with them?

He sat up. "That's not a problem, is it?"

"Well, I wasn't planning on anything obvious like throwing you down on the breakfast table and having my way with you—"

"That's a shame."

"—but I've never excelled at keeping secrets."

"You work in the medical field. Doctor-patient confidentiality is standard, right? Can this be employer-therapist confidentiality?"

Actually, she preferred not to dwell on the fact that she was sleeping with the guy who signed her paychecks. In that context, it seemed unsavory.

"She's a kid who just got dumped," he continued. "Finding out about our getting together days after Aaron broke her heart would be cruel timing."

"I guess you're right." No point in rubbing salt in Vicki's emotional wounds.

"Thank you." His earnest gaze made it clear this was important to him. But after a moment, his expression turned playful. "I have some ideas about how I can demonstrate my gratitude." The seductive drawl in his voice brightened her mood considerably.

"Yeah?" She reached for him. "Like what, exactly?"

As he began whispering his very detailed plans, they both forgot all about dessert, their only hunger for each other.

As soon as the dinner dishes had been cleared away on Tuesday, Sierra declared, "Game night! Participation is mandatory." She delivered the announcement with a smile to make herself seem like less of a dictator, but no way was she letting Vicki disappear into her room for the remainder of the evening.

With the exception of two hours today at the weekly festival meeting, where Vicki had been as animated as any of the other women on the committee, she'd been fairly subdued since her friends left Sunday. Sierra was determined to keep the young woman engaged. Plus, structured evening activities for the three of them kept Sierra from counting the minutes until bedtime. Last night, Jarrett had appeared in her doorway to kiss her good-night. Which had taken three hours. So far, rain had made stargazing impossible. Luckily, the forecast for this weekend's festival was clear. She just hoped the ground had dried sufficiently by then so that the Rosses weren't hosting the first annual Harvest Day mud pit.

"Game night?" Vicki echoed disdainfully. "What is with you and the days-of-yore quality time? Last night, it was a jigsaw puzzle—"

"I'm still bitter we turned out to only have 1,499 pieces of a 1,500-piece puzzle," Sierra fumed.

"And now board games? Throw in some paper dolls and blue hair rinse, and you'd be the little old lady my parents used to hire to babysit me."

Undeterred, Sierra plopped the Monopoly box she'd pulled from the hall closet onto the table. "So, basically, what you're saying is you don't want to play because you know I'll win?"

Vicki narrowed her eyes. "Big talk for a woman who's about to get her ass kicked. I'll be the banker."

Jarrett unfolded the board, holding out the silver tokens in his palm so everyone could choose what they wanted to be.

"I'm the hat," Sierra said.

Jarrett set two pieces on Go. "And I've got dibs on the guy riding the horse, obviously. Vic?"

"I'll be the wheelbarrow. Closest thing to a wheelch— Wait, screw that. Give me the race car."

An hour later, Jarrett was smirking from behind a pile of money. Vicki didn't have quite as much cash, but, since she'd amassed far more property than her brother, she didn't have reason to worry yet. Meanwhile, luck had not favored Sierra, who'd landed in jail three times.

"These freaking dice are cursed," she muttered, preparing to roll them again.

"Sore loser," Vicki said.

"Hell yes," Sierra agreed, tossing the dice. She moved her token around the corner of the board, growling in frustration. There were only two spaces that already had hotels, but she had to land on one of them?

Jarrett didn't own much, but his strategy of investing everything he had was paying off. "Looks like someone can't afford the rent," he singsonged.

"Only because my employers don't pay me what I'm worth." Since she had no properties of her own, she couldn't even mortgage them to complete her turn.

Jarrett's teasing gaze dropped slowly over her, and her skin warmed at the memory of his touch. "Maybe we can work out some kind of trade for services."

Vicki whipped her head around. "Ew."

He raised an eyebrow. "I was going to ask her to bake more of those caramel brownies. Get your mind out of the gutter."

"I might as well make brownies. I'm done here." She tossed the top-hat token back into the box and pushed her chair away from the table.

"Guess it comes down to you and me," he challenged his sister. "To the victor go the brownies!"

She rolled her eyes. "You can't eat a whole pan by yourself."

"Shows what you know," he said, reaching for the dice. "I am a man of insatiable appetites."

Sierra poked her head into the pantry to hide her smile. Jarrett's insatiability was why their lovemaking had gone on for hours last night. He'd been teasing about going to his room for more condoms when she'd fallen asleep limp, exhausted and thoroughly sated in his arms. *But I'm wide-awake now.* She darted a glance at the clock.

All right, so she'd failed to avoid the bedtime countdown. But she awarded herself points for temporarily delaying it. That qualified as willpower. Almost.

SETUP FOR THE Harvest Day Festival began on Friday after lunch. The entire festival committee showed up, many women accompanied by husbands and brothers to assist with the manual labor. Kate had both Will and teenage Luke with her.

"Cole said he'll stop by once he's off duty if we still need him," she told Sierra. She consulted the binder in her hand with a worried sigh. "We could be at this all night."

"I don't know." Sierra was less daunted by the workload. "Between Vicki and Becca, they have the troops whipped into shape and executing their orders with precision."

Vicki was stationed on the porch with half of a two-way radio set, signing in volunteers and surveying the landscape. Meanwhile, Becca Johnston, armed with the other radio receiver, was zipping around the ranch like a hummingbird that had just downed its first espresso. Sierra's theory was that the woman was moving too fast to be seen by the naked eye; the brain just filled in an image every time it detected the hot pink of her shirt flit by.

Jarrett was down by the stables, where pony rides would be offered in the small practice ring tomorrow. Goats and a friendly pig would make up a temporary petting zoo in the bigger ring. Sierra was relieved he wasn't anywhere in her vicinity, lest Kate see them together and somehow deduce their affair. The blonde's detecting skills were every bit as honed as her policeman fiancé's. At the committee lunch on Tuesday, Carrie Ann Rhodes, who was in her second trimester, said Kate had figured out she was pregnant before Carrie Ann had even taken the test.

"Kate?" A woman at the base of the hill cupped her mouth and yelled up to them. "Anita just got the sound system into the tent and says we're missing some cables. You happen to know where they are?"

"I'm on it." Kate headed in that direction at the same time a truck pulling a long trailer approached the house.

Sierra went to meet the driver to let him know Vicki had everyone's assignments. Three men climbed down from the mud-spattered cab.

The driver's eyes widened when he saw her. "And who might you be, little lady?" One of his companions ogled her outright, while the younger one ducked his gaze with a quick, deferential tip of his ball cap in greeting.

"Sierra Bailey, festival volunteer, physical therapist and ornery cuss who doesn't appreciate being called 'little.'"

The man laughed, nearly good-looking if it weren't for the tobacco-stained teeth. "Well, I'm Larry Breelan. This is my brother Daryl and my other brother, Grady. We've got the risers for the tent." He winked at her. "The Harvest Queen pageant is our favorite event of the whole festival."

She jerked a thumb over her shoulder. "You'll need to see Vicki about unloading the risers and anything else she needs your help with. Don't give her any crap, and there's fresh-squeezed lemonade and homemade brownies in your future."

"You can count on us."

Not only did she end up supplying snacks for the volunteers, the ranch was still bustling with volunteers by dinner.

"I took care of it," Vicki told her, rubbing the back of her neck. "The local pizza parlor is bringing us twenty pepperoni pies in exchange for special advertising at the festival tomorrow and preferential booth location."

Sierra leaned against the porch railing, regarding her with admiration. "I don't know what your major is, but you could have a future as some kind of events coordinator. You've done a fantastic job today." She hesitated, wondering if she should suggest the girl go inside and rest for a little while. She looked beat.

"What?" Vicki glared.

"I didn't say anything."

"You had that expression like you were about to ask me how I'm doing. That's been the only thing I've hated about today, the constant questioning of how I'm doing. I'm *fine*."

Sierra held her hands up in front of her. "All right, no need to bite my head off. Just make sure you save some reserve energy for tomorrow. That's when the real work is."

"Nah. Tomorrow will be fun. Sunday is the part that will suck." Vicki screwed up her face, looking like a four-year-old who'd just been served a plate of broccoli. "Cleanup."

"Yikes. I hadn't thought that far ahead."

"Well, now that you've been warned, plan accordingly. Stay hydrated, take your vitamins, that kind of thing." She gave Sierra an assessing look. "You probably shouldn't stay up too late tonight."

Was there a hidden meaning in that? Sierra's stomach knotted. Did Vicki somehow know that Sierra's past few nights hadn't been all that restful? *Oh, hell, what if we've been making too much noise?* That was a mortifying thought. Then again, maybe the effort of keeping a secret was just making Sierra paranoid. She could be reading too much into Vicki's suggestion.

"I'll be sure to get plenty of sleep," she said, striving for a casual tone. "You do the same."

Before Vicki could answer, her walkie-talkie crackled.

"Victoria? Becca here. Holt Miller has a question for you."

Sierra took that as her cue to leave.

All of the people who were still present when the pizzas arrived expressed heartfelt gratitude and undying devotion to Vicki. Cole Trent teasingly asked her if she had ever thought about a future as an elected official.

"Mayor Victoria Ross," he said, reaching for the soda he'd set on the porch railing. "Something to consider a decade or two down the road."

Kate and Cole were the last ones to leave. By the time they drove away, Vicki was nodding off in her chair. Sierra helped with her pre-bedtime routine and didn't leave her alone until she was actually tucked in, sticking around longer than usual in case Vicki needed her for anything.

Now I just need someone to help me *to bed.* Stifling a yawn, Sierra tried to muster the oomph necessary to climb the spiral staircase. With slow, shuffling steps, she made her way to the top. Jarrett met her on the landing, toweling off his damp hair.

"You look as beat as I feel," he said sympathetically.

"Never tell a woman she looks tired."

"Okay. But when you catch sight of yourself in the mirror, don't say I didn't warn you." He wrapped his arms around her and kissed her on top of the head. "I'm assuming that we, by mutual agreement, are far too tired to fool around."

"I'd nod, but I don't have the energy."

He chuckled. "Don't worry. I'll leave you be tonight."

It was on the tip of her tongue to ask if he wanted to come join her in the giant bed anyway, just to sleep. Lord knew there was room enough for the both of them, and she liked waking up in his arms. But would his spending the night with sex removed from the equation be too much like a relationship? Was she attaching more significance to whatever was happening between them than actually existed?

Don't overcomplicate matters.

That was sound advice. Right up there with, don't pick a night when she had only half a brain cell awake to ponder whether the connection between her and Jarrett was a bona fide relationship...and whether she'd done something as crazy as fall in love.

THE MORNING OF the festival came way too early, but at least it was sunny and warm. After helping Vicki get out of bed and do a quick series of exercises, Sierra fortified herself with an extra-strong cup of coffee and prepared to enjoy her first Cupid's Bow festival.

Also, your last, she thought as she pulled on her boots.

Not necessarily. This town wasn't the mystical Brigadoon; Cupid's Bow wouldn't disappear for a hundred years once she crossed outside its borders. Texas might be a large state, but she could still come back for occasional visits. Kate had been hinting that she expected Sierra to be present for her wedding.

Jarrett, on the other hand, had never said a word about her returning. She supposed she should appreciate that he wasn't putting any pressure on her when her future was still undecided, but she wouldn't mind knowing that he wanted to see her again. She had fewer than ten days left here. When she was gone, would he simply forget about her?

Sierra didn't know if she'd see him again when her job on the ranch had ended. But she knew it would be a long damn time before she could ever forget him.

For now, however, she needed to push aside these questions. She and Jarrett were supposed to work together this morning, overseeing games of traditional cowboy skill. Becca had set up "horse" races, which would take place after the participating children decorated pool-noodle ponies with eyes, ears, manes and tails. There would also be rawhide braiding, lassoing and a station where each kid could design a brand and color it in marker onto a balloon cow.

But before she headed for her post, she needed to help set Vicki up at the tent where various events would take place throughout the day. After everyone had gone last night, Vicki had flatly reiterated that she had no intention of being "stuck on the porch all day while the rest of the town has a good time." Sierra went back to Vicki's room to make sure she was ready, and she gasped aloud at the sight of her patient taking a few stumbling steps away from her wheelchair.

"What are you *doing*?" Sierra demanded, rushing to her side just as she toppled. They'd discussed how important it was that her progress be done with Sierra's or Manuel's assistance. Without proper supervision, she could reinjure herself.

"Walking." Face pale, Vicki accepted her help back into the chair but her glower suggested she would bat away Sierra's hand if she could.

"Determination is good," Sierra said, "but only when paired with intelligent choices. You didn't even have a walker or crutch handy! Do you know how much a fall could set you back?"

"Maybe I only fell because you startled me," she said mulishly.

"You're smart enough to know that isn't true— momentary stupidity notwithstanding."

"I want to be able to go down the steps to my own house!" Vicki complained. "I want to participate in the cake walk. I want to be able to dance with a cute guy tonight." She huffed out a breath. "Did I tell you about my new positive visualization image?"

"No." But Sierra had figured it was no longer dancing with Aaron.

"It's me marching across campus, looking killer, finding Aaron and kicking him in the shin. Hard."

Well. It was a goal.

They got Vicki to the appropriate location, and Sierra mentally crossed her fingers that the surly girl would rediscover her people skills as the day wore on. She also hoped she regained her common sense. Should she ask someone like Kate to surreptitiously check in from time to time and make sure Vicki wasn't attempting to foolishly leave her wheelchair?

You already gave her the lecture. You can't be there for her twenty-four hours a day. The Rosses would be home in less than two weeks. Vicki wouldn't even be Sierra's patient anymore. In the meantime, if the teenager did take ill-advised risks, at least there was a first-aid booth nearby.

The festival hadn't officially started yet, so the first wave of visitors hadn't arrived on the flatbed trailer. But a lot of the volunteers getting set up had brought their families with them, so about half a dozen kids were gathered near the barn already. A teenager was distributing pellets to feed to the goats while Anita Drake and another woman were blowing up black-and-white Holstein-patterned balloons.

The children not playing with balloons or goats were watching Jarrett show off some roping tricks. He was spinning a lariat in a wide loop, jumping from side to side through it. The kids were laughing at his silly running commentary while the women working with balloons were sighing over his muscles and agility. Who could blame them for their sighs? It was difficult to imagine a man more appealing than a gorgeous cowboy who was good with children.

Especially one who moves like that, she thought appreciatively, her gaze following him. She wished she could walk straight up to him and kiss him good morning.

"Morning." He shoved his hat back on his head,

giving her a wide smile. "Everyone say hi to Miss Sierra. She's exactly the person we need for our next demonstration."

A couple of the kids dutifully chorused, "Hi, Miss Sierra."

"Demonstration?" she asked. Their job was to guide kids through turns trying to rope posts. But Jarrett could have started that without her. Especially since she didn't know the first thing about lassoing. Her part was more crowd control, keeping an eye on kids in line to make sure no one started any fights. Or wandered off and ended up spooking the skittish mare in the stable.

He came over to where she stood. "You guys want to see a demonstration, right?" Taking her hand, he led Sierra to the center of the ring. Under his breath, he said, "Don't worry—your part is easy. And maybe much, much later, I can show you some of my favorite grown-up rope maneuvers."

She refused to encourage him by grinning. "Pervert," she whispered.

He winked at her. Then he backed away, holding the rope up and telling the kids about the different parts of the lasso and showing them how the honda knot was used to control the size of the loop. "When you throw, you aim with the tip. Bring your arm over your head and turn your wrist, keeping a good momentum and the loop open. Then when you're ready, you throw it like you would a baseball." He crooked his arm forward and the spinning loop came sailing toward her.

The kids cheered when it dropped over her, and Sierra laughed. A month ago, she couldn't have imagined willingly spending a day on a ranch. Now she was voluntarily riding horses and being used for lasso practice.

As more festival guests arrived, the number of children grew. Jarrett stopped demonstrating tricks and began handing them smaller lariats. Before long, Sierra was busy distributing small prizes for the kids who managed to rope a post and cheerfully consoling those who hadn't accomplished it yet. Spirits were high and no one seemed too discouraged by failure.

Behind her, Sierra heard a woman say, "Oh, no, honey, I think you're too little."

Sierra turned and saw a woman with wavy brown hair surrounded by the cutest little cowgirls on the ranch. Three identical toddlers stood with their mom in denim vests and matching pink dresses. They each wore a different colored hat, and the one in green was gesturing enthusiastically toward Jarrett.

"How about we go feed the animals instead?" her mom suggested.

"Not to undermine your authority," Sierra said, "but I think maybe our lasso expert could give her a hand if she wants a try."

The pretty brunette smiled. "Thanks. That would be sweet." Her other two cowgirls were hiding behind their mom's legs as she talked to Sierra. Obviously, the one in the green hat was the bold risk-taker of the group.

Sierra grinned inwardly. *My kind of kid.* "Hold on a sec." She informed Jarrett of the situation and he walked over to the triplets.

"Hi, I'm Jarrett." He shook the mom's hand.

"Megan Rivers. And these are my girls. Daisy was hoping to take a turn with the lasso, but—"

He dropped down to the little girl's level, and something inside Sierra melted. He tapped the brim of the toddler's cowgirl hat. "I like your hat. Is green your favorite color?"

She eyed him as if taking his measure, then shook her head. "Purple."

"Well, I don't have any purple lassos—only boring plain ones—but would you like to try one anyway?"

"Yes!"

"Mind if I pick you up?"

The girl immediately thrust her arms toward him, zero hint of shyness in her personality. Jarrett took her to the center of the ring. Keeping the girl balanced on his hip, he held the rope with a lot of slack, handing her only the looped end to whirl around. She hit herself in the face with it once. Sierra couldn't hear what Jarrett said to her, but whatever it was made the little girl giggle.

"Okay, on three we're going to toss it over the post," he said. "One, two…*three*." As he said the last word, he charged forward, carrying the girl right up to the post, where she dropped the loop over the wood.

She responded with a joyful belly laugh, and several of the kids waiting in line applauded.

"Uh-oh," Megan said. "Now that he's set the example, he's going to have little ones asking to be picked up for the whole rest of the day."

Sierra suspected she was right. "Good thing he has strong arms."

Jarrett returned the little girl to her mother, who thanked him profusely before herding her girls toward another section. He watched the woman go with a bemused expression.

"What is it?" Sierra asked, battling a twinge of

envy. The triplets' mom was extremely pretty. And *she* wasn't moving away in a week or so.

"She did say her name was Megan, right? Megan Rivers? That's Will's neighbor." He lowered his voice to a confiding tone. "He said she was a thoroughly disagreeable woman and that he's never seen her smile."

"Really?" Sierra craned her head, staring after the woman. "She seemed perfectly nice to me."

"Me, too. Either Will's crazy or she just plain doesn't like him."

"Weird. Will's a great guy. Total charmer."

"Careful, darlin'." Jarrett leaned close with a mock growl. "Last time I got jealous of you and Will, I dragged you out of a dance hall to kiss you senseless."

She laughed at his edited version of events. "That's the worst threat I've ever heard in my life. I've been wanting to kiss you for over an hour."

He groaned. "Becca scheduled breaks for us, right?"

"Becca is superhuman. I'm not sure she believes in breaks."

Behind them, another child was calling for Jarrett's help.

"Better get back to work, cowboy."

"How am I supposed to focus when you're standing here being distractingly beautiful?"

She grinned. "I suppose I could find Will Trent and see if he needs my help."

Jarrett gave her such a heated look that for a breathtaking moment, she thought he might actually stake his claim by kissing her right there and then. He settled for a drawled warning. "We are going to have words later, Miss Sierra."

She couldn't wait.

Chapter Fourteen

Jarrett smiled gratefully as Anita Drake handed him a glass of ice-cold lemonade. The day had got warm. "Thank you."

"Least I could do after you generously let us use the ranch for the festival. Will you get a chance to eat lunch?"

"Yeah." He checked his watch. "Deputy Thomas is supposed to take over for me in a few minutes, long enough for me to eat." He'd sent Sierra off to get some food for herself, though, and to check on Vicki. At the thought of his sister, guilt twisted inside him. He hated lying to her about Sierra. He'd never discussed his love life much with Vic—those weren't appropriate conversations to have with his little sister—but now he was surprised to find himself wishing he could share how happy Sierra made him. *A selfish wish.* The last thing Vicki would want to hear about in the wake of her breakup was that Jarrett was happier than he deserved to be.

Jarrett's stomach growled, adding physical discomfort to his conflicted mental state. Thankfully, being punctual was one of the deputy's trademark qualities. Deputy Thomas arrived and Jarrett decided to head for whatever food vendor had the shortest line. A large family over by the Smoky Pig booth got their food and stepped away, drastically reducing the crowd in front of the order window. Jarrett quickly jumped in the line.

"Hey, J-Ross." Larry Breelan walked up behind him. "We don't see much of you in town lately."

"I've been busy working the ranch."

"Yeah—must be pulling double duty since your dad's attack. With you secluded out here, we were afraid the legendary Jarrett Ross love life had finally slowed down. End of an era. Should have known you're too smart for that, eh? Figured out how to swing it."

"What are you talking about?"

The man elbowed him. "Settle a bet between me and Grady. You're sleeping with that pretty redhead, aren't you? As soon as we saw her yesterday, I realized we'd been all wrong about your dry spell, that you—"

"Ms. Bailey is one hell of a physical therapist, and my family owes her a great debt for how much she's helped my sister. I would take any disrespectful comments about her *very* badly."

Larry shrank back, wide-eyed. "Well, hell, man, I didn't mean any disrespect. But we all know your track record with the ladies, and she's one mighty fine filly."

An involuntary snarl came from behind Jarrett's teeth.

"Sorry. I realize now I had the situation all wrong."

"You make sure to tell your brother that, too." Who else was speculating about Sierra? Probably anyone who knew his reputation. He was Jarrett Ross, and she was a beautiful woman sleeping down the hall from him every night. People would assume they were having sex.

Which you are. That was the worst part. Anyone gossiping about it would be right.

"Is anyone else speaking ill of Ms. Bailey?" he demanded.

Larry looked confused by the question. "Thinking that she knocked boots with you isn't an insult. More like, it makes her part of a club. You've been with half the ladies in town."

"I have not!" It was a blatant exaggeration, but he only had himself to blame for how people saw him. "You know, I just realized I'm not in the mood for barbecue." With a terse nod to Larry, he gave up his place in line.

Jarrett hated that anyone might think he'd hired Sierra based on her looks or with plans to seduce her. *Just like Vicki first thought.* He'd assured his sister that he would keep his distance from the therapist, and now he'd broken his promise.

His feelings for Sierra were different than anything he'd experienced before—he'd believed they were making *him* different. Better. But Breelan's words had been a reality check. Even knowing how important Sierra's professionalism was to her, Jarrett had slow-danced with her in public, kissed her outside the dance hall where they could have been seen. And now he was sneaking around behind his sister's back!

Vicki deserved more from him. And even though he knew he was making Sierra happy in the short run, maybe she deserved a better man.

"Hey." Sierra strolled into the stable, amused that there had been a time in the recent past when she'd had an aversion to being here. Now it was the source of some fond memories. She smiled at Jarrett, who was resting on a bale of hay with his long legs kicked out in front of him. "I was hoping to find you in here."

The sun had set an hour ago. The festival was still going strong, but most everyone was in the tent where the Harvest Queen had been crowned. There was live music and dancing. Although people seemed to be having fun, after the hectic frivolity of the day, Sierra was craving a little peace and quiet.

Be honest. Mostly, you're just craving him. They'd worked together all morning, but after lunch, it seemed as though every time she looked for Jarrett, he was suddenly needed elsewhere. Was it weird that, after only a few hours apart, she'd missed him? Not in some needy, codependent way. But every time something funny had happened, she'd automatically turned to joke with him about it—only to find that he wasn't there. And there'd been a few heart-melting moments with cute kids that she wished she could have seen his reaction to. The sight of him with Megan's little girl that morning remained a high point of her day.

"How was your afternoon?" she asked him now.

"Fine," he said, sparing her the briefest of glances. "Tiring."

She nodded in commiseration, walking over and cupping his shoulders with her hands. Stroking her fingers toward his neck, she applied light pressure to his scalene muscles. "Did you know I am trained in therapeutic massage? If you're sore, I can—"

He stood, the motion effectively knocking her

hands away. "Too bad I didn't know you when I was riding rodeo—talk about sore muscles. Today was a breeze compared to that."

She bit the inside of her lip, surprised at the rebuff. "All right." She wound her arms around his neck. "It was really just an excuse to touch you, anyway."

"Sierra." He backed away. "Someone might see."

Who, the horses? She resisted the urge to snap the question at him. She supposed it was possible that, in the event of a minor emergency, someone would come looking for the ranch owner. Regardless, Sierra had her pride—somewhat bruised for the rejection but still intact. She wasn't going to throw herself at an uninterested man.

But since when was Jarrett uninterested?

"Sorry," he said, his smile gentle. "But it would be really bad if Vicki heard about us from someone."

Then maybe we should tell her ourselves. But Vicki wasn't her sister, so she was deferring to his feelings on the matter. "Understood. I should go find her, anyway. Wish me luck persuading her she's had enough excitement for one day. See you back in the house?"

He nodded absently, but it was hours later before she heard him come up the stairs in the house. Pipes creaked, and she listened to the water run as he showered. If the situation were different, maybe she would have surprised him by joining him. After his strange mood in the stable, though, she was leaving it to him to make the next move.

Only, he didn't.

Once his shower was over, she held her breath, waiting to see if he appeared in her doorway as he had on previous nights. Instead, he padded to his room and closed the door, leaving her alone and perplexed and wondering what had gone wrong.

ON SUNDAY, IT took hours to deconstruct booths and haul away trash from the festival. Once it was all finished and Jarrett had again accepted the committee's thanks for use of the ranch, he locked himself away in the study on the pretext of having work to do. *You do have work you should be doing. You just aren't accomplishing any of it.*

His biggest accomplishment today was driving himself crazy by staying away from Sierra. How long did he think he could successfully avoid her?

Too restless to sit, he paced behind the desk. Even now, he wanted to go to her, tell her how much he'd missed her for the past two nights. But every time he thought of Larry Breelan's lewd expression, the knowing chuckle in the man's voice when he'd basically congratulated Jarrett on scoring with her...

So he stayed in the office, knowing he would crack eventually and need to touch her again, yet postponing the inescapable moment of weakness. When his phone rang, he answered it gratefully, thrilled to have a legitimate distraction.

"Hello?"

"Jarrett! How are you?" his mother asked. The happiness in her voice made her sound like almost a different person than the one who'd stood in this very room and told him she and Gavin needed time away. The trip to Tahoe had done her a lot of good.

"I'm..." Conflicted. Miserable. Weak-willed. "...great. We got everything all cleaned up from the festival today, restoring order to the ranch. So, no worries, the Twisted R you come home to will be in the same condition as when you left." The ranch might be the same, but *he* felt irrevocably changed by the past few weeks.

"Oh. Good." His mother's voice took on a dull note whenever the ranch came up.

He sighed. "You really aren't looking forward to being back here, are you?"

"It's not that. Exactly. The Twisted R is my home, but— Of course I can't wait to see you and your sister again. She texted me a picture earlier today of her standing! That Sierra you hired must be a godsend. I'm sorry she'll be leaving so shortly after our return. I'd like to get to know her better, thank her properly for her help."

"Yeah, well." His throat burned, and he had trouble getting the words out. "She'll be moving on to other folks who need her." Her interview in Fort Worth was scheduled for Tuesday. She was driving up that morning and wouldn't be back until sometime on Wednesday. He felt confident that the people at the clinic would offer her the job. They'd be fools not to.

Just like you're a fool for letting her go. He scowled. What choice did he have? She'd never really been his to hold on to in the first place.

WHEN SIERRA CAME into the kitchen on Monday to fix lunch, there was a napkin sitting on the table. The words *Go riding with me?* had been written across it in bright marker. A gesture from Jarrett? Had she misinterpreted his aloof demeanor over the past two days?

Maybe being drained from all the festival-related activities had just left him cranky. Or maybe it was all the extra pairs of eyes on the ranch this weekend that had prompted him to keep his distance. She supposed she understood, but it stung, feeling like his sordid secret, unfit for acknowledging during daylight hours.

"Thought I heard you in here," he said from behind her as she filled a pot with water for boiling pasta. "Did you get my invitation?"

She glanced toward the napkin on the counter, her mouth lifting in a half smile. "On the traditional Jarrett Ross stationery."

"I should really shop for matching envelopes." He looked thoughtful. "Maybe I could origami one out of a paper towel."

She laughed, feeling some of the strain that had plagued her since Saturday finally ease.

"So. Can you go riding with me this afternoon, or do you and Vicki have plans?"

"Just the opposite. I'm trying to get her to take it easy after an eventful weekend. She's doesn't appreciate my caution, though."

The girl seemed mad at her. She hadn't said much during the dinner they'd eaten in Jarrett's absence last night, but every once in a while, Sierra would catch Vicki looking at her with a displeased expression on her face. *Because she thinks I'm slowing down her progress?* Or was it something else?

Sierra sighed. "I guess I should remind her about her promise to be a model patient if I braved riding a horse." That gave her an idea of how to get back into the girl's good graces. She made a mental note to ask Manuel at Vicki's appointment Thursday about getting Vicki back into the saddle. Maybe that was something Sierra could help her accomplish before—

"You okay?" Jarrett asked. "I didn't realize she was giving you that much trouble."

"Oh, I can handle Vicki. I was just thinking how few days I have left here."

"Yeah." He looked away, his expression despondent.

Perhaps that explained his recent detachment. Was he just trying to prepare himself for their goodbye? It was nice to think he was so affected by the idea of her leaving, proving that he cared.

"I'd love to go riding with you," she said impulsively.

During lunch, she told Vicki about their plans and promised she'd ask Manuel this week what needed to be done for Vicki to ride again. The announcement didn't elicit quite the celebration she'd hoped for, but at least her patient wasn't actively glaring at her. After they ate, Vicki put in a DVD. Sierra promised she'd be back by the time the movie was over and that they'd work more on taking actual steps with the crutches. The new goal was for Vicki to walk up to her parents when they returned next week. It would be a lovely homecoming gift.

Down at the stables, Sierra helped with tacking up the horses, although Jarrett double-checked her work to make sure everything was secure.

"Nice job," he praised her. "If we had more time, I bet I could turn you into a first-rate horsewoman."

If we had more time... A pang went through her at all the ways that sentence could end. Not having more practice saddling horses wouldn't be what she regretted most when she left.

"We'll be going a bit off the usual trail today," he

warned as they led the horses out of the stable. "I have something I want to show you."

Twenty minutes later, they passed through a copse of peach trees, where she mocked his constantly having to duck branches—"Finally, a bonus to being this short!"—and emerged in a small clearing. The house that sat in front of them was too oblong to be rightly called a cottage, but there was something charming about it nonetheless. Two untrimmed rosebushes flanked the front door, the flowers growing in fragrant profusion.

"What's this?" she asked as they dismounted.

Jarrett secured the horses to a hitching post. "The bunkhouse." He held the door open for her.

It was a little musty inside, the sunlight through the window illuminating the dust motes that danced in the air. The back wall was all stonework, full of rustic charm, but that was about all she could say for the decor. There was little furniture and even less style. A folding card table sat in the kitchen with two sturdy but mismatched chairs.

"Tell me the truth—you only brought me here so we could fool around with no chance of Vicki catching on." It was supposed to have been a teasing comment, but there was an aggressive undertone to her words.

He blinked, obviously hearing it, too. "We agreed it was best if she didn't know about us."

More like, you *agreed.* "Maybe we should revisit that. I think she's suspicious that something's going on."

"She'd be suspicious anyway." Shoving a hand through his hair, he turned to gaze out a grimy window. "Even when I first hired you, she thought I had ulterior motives. Not only would telling her be hurtful timing, it would lower her opinion of me even more."

The recrimination in his tone reminded her of the night he'd told her about Vicki's accident, and she tried to lighten the mood. "Being drawn to me isn't a character flaw—it's just good taste."

He didn't respond, and she rested her cheek against his back. She still thought they should tell Vicki, but Sierra wasn't the one who would have to deal with any fallout from the conversation if it was the wrong decision.

He turned, wrapping her in his arms. Despite the momentary tension between them, it felt so good for him to be holding her again. "The real reason I brought you here was so you could see my future home. Obviously, it needs lots of TLC."

"But it has great potential," she said. All it took was some imagination to see what could be created. She admired his willingness to make the effort. Anyone in her family would probably take one look around and declare the place unfit for habitation. But a house didn't need thousand-dollar artwork and a three-car garage to be an inviting home.

"I want to completely remodel the bathroom," he told her, drawing her to the other end of the house for a quick tour. "I'm thinking whirlpool tub. The bedroom just needs some minor floor repair where the hardwood's warped and, obviously, furniture." He gave her a lopsided grin. "Maybe I'll ask my parents if I can take the king bed from the guest room. It's really too big for that room anyway, and I've developed a real fondness for that bed."

Desire rippled through her as she recalled the many delicious things he'd done to her there.

She couldn't imagine that the brick fireplace in the living room would be used often in the Texas heat, yet the image of snuggling in this high-ceilinged room in front of the flames was undeniably cozy. Her eyes prickled with sudden tears she refused to shed. She was touched that Jarrett had wanted to show her the future he was mapping out, yet knowing she wouldn't be part of that future hurt more than it should.

"...and a huge flat-screen TV," he was saying. "Seriously, huge. I mean, this is Texas, right? Go big or go home. And in here," he added, as they reached the kitchen, "I was thinking... Honestly, I have no idea. Most of my culinary skills center around coffeemakers and grills."

She laughed. "Well, coffee is the most important meal of the day."

He brushed his index finger over her lips. "I've missed your smile." A wave of anticipation went through her as he bent closer, cupping her face. "And I've missed doing this."

His mouth met hers in a kiss that started out as sweet reunion but ignited into something more arousing. Deepening their kiss, he dropped his hands to her butt and pulled her against him.

She unbuttoned the top of his shirt, kissing the exposed column of his throat. "I want you so much."

He walked them backward until he hit a chair, and she straddled his lap, their kisses frenzied. She had to get back to the house soon, and they didn't waste any time. Buttons and zippers were dealt with impatiently, and she almost laughed in wry frustration.

It was a lot easier to remove pajamas than jeans and boots. But, between them, they managed. Jarrett was wearing only a condom when he tugged her forward, her unbuttoned shirt hanging loose at her sides. She slowly lowered herself over him, her breath hitching as he cupped her breasts, rubbing the tight peaks. She tightened her inner muscles around him, and he groaned her name.

It occurred to her that they didn't have to worry about being quiet, and when her climax rolled through her, she threw back her head with a cry of joy.

Afterward, she rested her head on his shoulder, her smile bittersweet. She'd finally got her wish—no longer only a guilty pleasure he saved for the wee hours of the night but his lover in the full light of day. She wished she could stay here, spend an idyllic afternoon in his arms, but she had to go. They were out of time.

ALL THROUGH SIERRA's interview on Tuesday, she mentally chided herself for being too subdued. *They'll think you aren't excited about the opportunity.* But her worries turned out to be unfounded. Perhaps having a quieter demeanor was the key to seeming like a reserved professional, because by the time the clinic closed for the day, they'd offered her the job.

I should be happy about this, she told herself as she reached out to shake hands with the woman who'd led the interview. Fort Worth wasn't far from Dallas, which would make relocating easier. The pay was competitive for her field, and the people seemed nice enough—although, only time would tell whether they liked outspoken, headstrong Sierra once they got to know her. The Sierra in today's interview had been a well-behaved doppelgänger.

"Are you headed to a hotel?" the HR manager asked. "We'd be happy to take you to dinner and answer any other questions you might have."

"Thank you, but if you don't mind, I'll take a rain check," Sierra said. "I have a lot to mull over."

"Of course." The manager nodded approvingly. "You have a big decision to make."

After grabbing a salad from an upscale deli, Sierra checked into a hotel room, ostensibly to think about her career. So why was she staring at the generic hotel wall art of a cowboy silhouetted on a horse and thinking only of the cowboy back in Cupid's Bow? She pulled out her phone and texted him that the job was hers if she wanted it, and they'd love for her to start next week.

Ten minutes later, she received the single-word response: Congratulations.

She checked the phone twice more to see if he'd added anything else, but, really, what was there to say? They'd both known from day one that she was looking for a new place to land, and now she'd found it. Congratulations, indeed.

A month ago, being by herself for the night would have seemed perfectly normal, but now loneliness gripped her. *Because it's too quiet in here.* She turned on the television, flipping past news and sports and stopping just long enough on a fashion reality show to watch the judges determine the week's winner. After that, she got bored and reached for her phone.

She could always call Jarrett. He might have more to say during an actual conversation than in a text.

But she couldn't bring herself to dial his number. It felt too needy. If she couldn't survive one night without him, what was she going to do about the coming nights and weeks and months? That thought made her stomach churn, and she scrolled through her contact list in sudden desperation.

"Hello?"

"Hi, Mom." Sierra hoped the warble in her voice wasn't so pronounced through their connection.

"Sierra! How wonderful to hear from you, darling. I don't have long—your father and I are headed for a benefit tonight—but tell me everything. How's the job search?"

"I got an offer in Fort Worth today." She proceeded to tell her mom all about the clinic and the neighborhood it was in. Sierra planned to drive around a little bit and check into living arrangements before she returned to Cupid's Bow tomorrow. If she took this job, the clinic wanted her to start soon, so finding a place was top priority.

After chatting about that for a bit, conversation turned to her brother's wedding plans. Muriel was still obsessing over every detail. "Apparently, Kyle and Annabel didn't discuss much of this before he proposed, so there's a lot to hash out. But it's good that they're learning to argue respectfully and resolve differences. It takes compromise to make a marriage work. I know you probably think compromising is a sign of weakness—"

"No, I don't. I could make some compromises, for the right person." But how did you know when you'd found the right person—the one who would be worth the effort? *I love Jarrett.* She'd suspected it for days but had known it in her heart after he'd made love to her yesterday and she'd spent her entire walk back to the house trying not to cry.

She loved him, but she was uncertain what his feelings were. He'd admitted that, in the past, he'd had very shallow relationships. Was it arrogant to think that she was different, that she was special to him?

As she ended the call with her mother, Sierra knew that, if Jarrett asked, she would be willing to make some compromises in order to keep seeing him. But, so far, he hadn't cared enough to ask.

Chapter Fifteen

Passing the sign that said Welcome to Cupid's Bow gave Sierra an overwhelming sense of déjà vu. Had it been only a few weeks ago that she'd packed up her car and driven into this town with a sense of foreboding? She'd wondered if she could survive the isolation of the Twisted R for so long, but the time had flown.

Speaking of time. Battling back the emotion that had kept trying to well up, she glanced at her clock. She'd told Jarrett she wasn't sure when she'd be back. Given the approaching dinner hour, maybe she should call and see whether he was already cooking something or if he wanted her to pick up some food in town.

The phone rang so many times that she'd almost given up hope anyone would answer when she heard Vicki's voice.

"Hello?"

"Hey, it's Sierra. I'm back—just crossed the town line. I thought I'd see if your brother was already in the middle of making dinner."

"Ha! He's barricaded himself in the study. He is in a serious *mood*. I think it stresses him out to be left alone with me."

"Were you being difficult?"

"He hasn't spoken to me enough to give me the chance."

"Then it's probably something else. Worries about hay or straw or grass seed or something." He'd once launched into a discussion of grass at dinner that had lasted a full half hour. Sierra had managed not to fall asleep, but only because she'd entertained herself by mentally replaying her favorite episode of an old sitcom.

"He could be grumpy because he misses you."

Sierra wanted to believe that, but she refused to cling to false hope. "You mean because he misses my cooking? I doubt my being gone had much impact. I was only away overnight."

"Then maybe he missed you last night. Tell me the truth—are you sleeping with my brother?"

She gripped the steering wheel, too startled to answer. Her natural impulse was to be candid, but that wasn't what Jarrett wanted. Honesty warred with loyalty. Meanwhile, the pause had stretched on so long, she feared it had become an answer all on its own.

She heard Vicki's intake of breath as she filled in the gap for herself.

Hell with it. If Sierra was going to get in trouble, she would do it by owning her actions, not letting a cowardly silence speak for her. "Yes. I am."

"I *knew* it. The two of you have been lying to me, and I knew it!" Judging from the pain in her voice, she'd been secretly hoping she was wrong.

Panic blossomed inside her. Oh, crap. She'd made the wrong choice, hadn't she? She'd betrayed Jarrett's wishes and, in the process, upset his sister. "Vicki, we—"

But the line was already dead.

JARRETT STARED AT the computer screen, but the jumble of numbers on the spreadsheet made no more sense to him now than they had the past twenty times he'd looked. He might as well be trying to read ancient hieroglyphics. The last thing he could remember clearly reading was Sierra's text yesterday saying that she'd been offered the job.

All was as it should be. She was an educated woman from a wealthy family. She should be building a successful career, not shacking up in some three-room bunkhouse with a cowboy whose reputation was a local joke. He thought of his mom, who tolerated life on the Twisted R for the sake of her family but didn't love the ranch, not the way Jarrett and his father did. Even if Sierra didn't have this opportunity in Fort Worth, how long could she have tolerated it here before realizing it wasn't where she belonged? *If you were a better man, you'd be happy for her.* But—

Something smashed against the office door, and he jumped in his chair. What the hell? He walked over to the door and opened it cautiously. One of his dad's Larry McMurtry novels lay on the floor. Vicki sat in her wheelchair a few feet away, her face red.

"Was that your version of knocking?" he asked, smoothing out the book's pages. When he realized how hard she was breathing, worry clutched at him. "Are you all right? Should I call a doctor, or—"

"I don't know which I hate more, that you slept with her or that you thought I was too stupid to notice! I'm crippled, not brain-dead."

The attack left him reeling. She'd found out about Sierra. His careful attempts to keep their relationship a secret had failed. "How do you know?"

"Because she told me! *She* had the balls to admit it, unlike you. What was it you said—that you didn't even see her as a woman? You are a liar, Jarrett. You still treat me like a dumb kid, like I don't have eyes in my head. You are so—"

"I know you're not a dumb kid. I've always wished I were as smart as you."

"Don't try to flatter or charm me! I'm not some rodeo groupie. In fact, don't speak to me at all." She turned for her room.

"Vic, we should talk about this."

"Yes, we *should* have. But you opted for lies and secrecy and patronizing your kid sister. So you'll just have to deal with the consequences."

ANY FAR-FETCHED HOPES that Vicki was indulging in the silent treatment and hadn't confronted her brother were dashed when Jarrett came storming out of the house the second Sierra parked her car.

His face was cold with fury, hardly recognizable. "How dare you! You went behind my back and—"

"I didn't set out to tell her." She sagged against the front of her car for support. "She asked me point-blank."

Should she remind him that, if he'd fostered a different kind of relationship with his sister, Vicki might have asked *him* instead? Never mind. Why poke the bear?

He rocked back on his heels, his scathing expression making it clear her explanation hadn't pacified him a bit. "How convenient. You've wanted to tell her from the very first night, and she handed you your chance. I wonder how many hints you had to drop to get that to happen."

"Are you insane?" Forget placating his temper. Now she was ticked. She marched up to him. The man might be built like a redwood, but she wasn't about to cower. "She caught me completely off guard, which is actually a little weird since I already *warned* you she was onto us. Just like I warned you that I don't keep secrets well! And I don't passive-aggressively 'hint.' I say what the hell I'm thinking. Maybe you could learn a lesson from me."

"About ignoring people's wishes?" he countered. "About crushing someone's feelings? You should have seen…" Some of the rage drained from him, leaving sadness in its wake. "It wasn't worth hurting her like that over some fling."

Some fling. The words landed like a blow. She pressed a hand to her stomach as if applying pressure could relieve the pain. Ridiculous. The agonizing throb she felt wasn't in her abdomen. It was in her heart. "That's all this was—a fling?"

"You're leaving next week, Sierra. What else could it be?" He said it so matter-of-factly that she wanted to cry.

Not in front of him. "You're absolutely right. About us, anyway. You're wrong about my leaving next week, though. I'll be gone on Thursday, as soon as I've taken Vicki to her PT appointment with Manuel. Maybe once I'm out of the house, you and Vicki can…" As much as she wanted to be a mature person, she couldn't choke back tears long enough to wish him and his sister well. Instead, she simply fled into the house and up the stairs.

Jarrett didn't follow. She'd known he wouldn't. And she supposed that gave her all the answer she'd ever needed about whether he was the right person and whether he'd fight to make a relationship work.

Then again, why should he? In his eyes, they'd never had a relationship.

"I CAN'T BELIEVE you're leaving," Kate sniffed.

Despite everything, that made Sierra laugh. "Seriously? Because I've been telling you since the day we met that I wasn't sticking around."

"I think I'm too depressed to even order dessert."

Sierra had said her goodbyes to the Rosses this morning. Since Vicki was only speaking in monosyllables and Jarrett wouldn't look at her, it hadn't taken long. But she'd promised to meet Kate at the Smoky Pig on her way out of town for one last lunch.

"Maybe you could ask for a dessert to go," Sierra suggested, "and eat it later, when you're feeling more chipper."

Kate gave her a hollow, sad-eyed look that suggested her soul would never know joy again.

"That might be overdoing it a little," Sierra said. "Come on. You have friends here! Lots of them. And you're going to marry the gorgeous town sheriff and mother his adorable twins, who worship you. My sympathy for you is limited."

"Oh, all right." Kate flipped open the dessert menu, even though she probably had it memorized. "But it still sucks that you're leaving."

"Try to be happy for me." *Someone has to be.* "I'm on to bigger and better things."

Some people would say that there was nothing bet-

ter than love. Sierra was less than impressed with
it. She'd finally fallen in love with someone—and
promptly had her heart broken. No wonder Vicki
wanted to walk up to Aaron and kick him in the shin.
Sierra had to admit that the idea of kicking a certain
cowboy was tempting. But what would be the point?
No matter where she kicked him, she couldn't hurt
Jarrett as much as he'd hurt her.

WITH SIERRA GONE, the house was eerily silent all of
Thursday night and into the next day. His parents
wouldn't get in until Saturday, and as he cooked dinner Friday night, Jarrett wondered if Vicki planned to
speak to him at all before then. What was she planning
to tell them about her seething hatred for her brother?

Maybe they wouldn't even notice. After all, it wasn't
much of a change from Vicki's attitude toward him
before they'd left. In that moment, he realized how
much progress had been made over the past couple of
weeks. Siding with Vicki in their no-liver ban, teaming
up with her to convince Sierra to give horseback riding another shot, laughing as Vicki won all his money
in a board game. With Sierra in the house, he and his
sister had begun to bond again.

*And you destroyed that bond by sleeping with her
therapist.*

Well, she was allowed to be mad at him, but she
wasn't allowed to starve herself. He turned off the
stove and went to her room, knocking on the door. As
expected, there was no answer, so he knocked more
forcefully.

"Vicki, you have to eat. I'm not going away until

you come out of there." He had all night and no place to be. He could out-stubborn her if necessary.

Huh. Maybe Sierra had rubbed off on him. He recalled the day he'd hired her, how he'd meekly honored Vicki's wishes not to be disturbed, but Sierra had insisted otherwise.

She'd been right that day. Had she been right when she'd goaded him to tell Vicki about their affair? *The last thing my nineteen-year-old sister wants to hear about is my sex life.* But what he felt for Sierra went far beyond sex.

He knocked again. "I'm gearing up to sing 'a hundred bottles of sarsaparilla on the wall.'" She wasn't old enough for beer. "I'll make it a thousand if I have to."

"If I eat," she asked from the other side of the door, "will you leave me in peace?"

"Yes." Maybe.

Dinner was grim, and the chicken was rubbery, but he counted it as a victory that she had joined him at the kitchen table.

"No offense," she said, wincing at a bite of overcooked broccoli, "but your cooking sucks. I miss Sierra."

Just hearing her name was wrenching. He pushed his own plate away. "I'm sorry she's gone."

Vicki stared at him, her gaze penetrating. "Are you? I heard you yelling at her the other night."

"Only because she upset you." Even as he said that, he knew where the blame belonged. "All right, I know I'm the one who really upset you. I promised I wouldn't get involved with her, but I did."

"And you *lied* about it." Vicki's wounded tone suddenly made him question what she was more upset about—his involvement with Sierra or that he'd kept it secret?

Oh, Lord. Had Sierra been right all along? "I didn't want you to know," he admitted. "You and Aaron had just broken up. I figured the last thing you needed was to be trapped in the house with a happy couple, and—"

"Happy couple?" Her eyes widened. "Is that what you were? Or was she just another playmate?"

He flinched but supposed there were worse terms she could have used. "You know Sierra. She was never 'just' anything."

"Then what the hell, dude? Why did you let her go out with Will Trent? Why did you let her leave us?"

"I'm confused." He rubbed his temples. "You *want* me and Sierra together?"

"If the two of you make each other happy…" She spread her arms wide and gave him a *duh* look.

He sat back in his chair, too moved to respond. It said a lot about Vicki's strength of character that she wanted his happiness after he'd been such a crappy brother. "Frankly, I wouldn't blame you if you hated me." The admission came out low and gravelly, and he hoped she heard it because he wasn't sure he could say it again.

She sighed heavily. "After my accident, you hated yourself enough for both of us. I didn't start out mad at you, specifically. There was just so *much* anger. I was ticked that I couldn't go back to school, that I had to lie in a hospital bed for weeks, that I couldn't—" Her voice caught, and her eyes shimmered with tears. "But it wasn't all anger. I was scared, too. Even though every doctor said I'd be able to walk again, it's hard to believe that when you can't even sit up."

The familiar guilt stabbed at him again, but this wasn't about him. This was about his sister. He squeezed his hand. "Vicki, I'm so sorry for what you've been through. If I could have done *anything* to spare you that pain..."

"Well." She swallowed hard. "At least now I know how tough I am. I've survived the worst of it."

"You're a badass."

"I'm a Ross. Now the question is, how much of a badass are you? Are you man enough to admit when you're wrong? Sierra's forgiven me plenty of times for being a butthead. If you talk to her—"

"It's almost better that she left angry. It made saying goodbye easier."

"But why does it have to be goodbye? You care about her."

"Enough to want what's best for her. I don't think I'm it." When Vicki opened her mouth to argue, he added, "And Cupid's Bow was never what she wanted for the long term. She joked about it all the time when she first got here, how uncivilized we were and how the movie theater only shows films from before 2010."

"Yeah, but maybe her feelings changed. Maybe 'the town' came to mean a lot to her." She stared at him pointedly to make sure he knew she wasn't talking about Cupid's Bow. "But you'll never know unless you ask."

SIERRA SAT ACROSS the desk from the director of the Sports Medicine Rehabilitation Program, trying to be a full participant in the conversation. After all, they were trying to decide where she'd fit best at the clinic, so she had a vested interest in the outcome.

"You haven't done much work specifically in sports medicine," the director observed. "What interests you about the program?"

"Your work with high school athletes. I recently worked very closely with a nineteen-year-old, and it got me to thinking about adolescents. Teenagers, neither adults nor typical pediatric patients, are uniquely challenging. But also uniquely rewarding." Less tactfully, they were pains in the ass—which was right in her wheelhouse.

Suddenly, she heard Kate Sullivan's teasing voice in her head. *I know I'm being a pain, but meddling is the Cupid's Bow way.* The citizens of Cupid's Bow were opinionated and nosy and interfered in each other's lives. Sierra fit right in.

The thought gave her a pang, and she felt irrational annoyance at Daniel Baron for leading her to Cupid's Bow in the first place. Before his email, she'd never even heard of the speck on the map. From the start, Cupid's Bow had been a temporary gig. It had been a way station for her, not a home.

Then why do I feel so homesick?

A month ago, Jarrett had stood in this room waiting for his mother, afraid of what bad news she might bring. Now both his parents were cuddled together on the other side of the desk—Gavin in his leather chair, Anne perched on the arm of the chair as they went over facts and figures from the past few weeks.

"You two certainly look cozy," he couldn't help

teasing. He was thrilled for them. He hadn't seen either of them this relaxed in a long time.

"Yes, well, Tahoe did us a world of good," Anne said.

"I've promised your mother we'll go back for two weeks out of every year," Gavin said. "Provided you don't mind being in charge while I'm gone."

"And *I* promised to quit bellyaching about everything around here." She looked around the room with a fond smile. "There are a lot of good memories in this house. I just need the break from time to time—and to know that your father loves me as much as he loves the ranch."

"More," Gavin said, suddenly serious. "So much more. Son, a word of advice from your old man? If you ever fall in love, make sure she knows it. Make sure you appreciate her and let her know every damn day how lucky you are."

The words resonated with him. He'd thought so often about what Sierra deserved in life...but didn't she deserve to know his feelings?

Maybe she didn't return them. Maybe she didn't belong in Cupid's Bow. Nonetheless, she was a strong advocate of the truth. And the truth was: he loved her. He wanted to tell her that face-to-face. As soon as possible.

His heart thudded wildly, like a stampede in his chest. "If you guys will excuse me, I have somewhere important I need to be." Fort Worth. He bolted from his chair, calling over his shoulder, "I may be gone a few days."

Not wanting to get their hopes up, he didn't add

that, if luck was with him, they'd be meeting their future daughter-in-law soon.

JARRETT DRUMMED HIS fingers on the side of his truck as he watched the number of gallons climb on the gas pump and impatiently waited for the tank to fill. He was so antsy to hit the road that he hadn't even bothered packing—he had a wallet, his phone and the spare toothbrush he kept in the glove compartment of his truck. *I'll buy anything else I need.*

Except, the one thing he really needed—Sierra's forgiveness—couldn't be purchased.

Maybe he should call her. After all, showing up in Fort Worth was a grand romantic gesture, but he had no idea how to track her down once he got there. Plus, he really, really needed to hear her voice after so many days apart.

He dialed, mentally crossing his fingers that she answered. If she wouldn't take his calls, he supposed that gave him some indication of how upset she was.

But she answered on the second ring, her voice puzzled. "Jarrett? Is Vicki okay?"

"Everything's fine." Well, there was the matter of the gaping emptiness in his life ever since she'd left, but hopefully they would fix that. "I'm calling to let you know that I'm coming to see you. Please don't try to talk me out of it, because I'm already on the way."

"You're what?" she asked, her voice strangled.

Damn. She really didn't sound happy to see him. "Sierra, I know you're probably still angry with me—"

"That is true. But we have other problems. Where are you, specifically?"

"The gas station just outside Cupid's Bow."

She started laughing, and he couldn't tell if the sound was joy or some kind of hysteria. "The one close to the hospital?"

"Yes. I haven't made it very far, but—"

"Good thing. I'm across the street."

"You're *where*?"

"I just finished an interview at the hospital. Manuel helped me set it up. Meet me in the main lobby?"

He closed the gas tank, back in his truck before she even finished her sentence.

When the hospital's automatic doors parted five minutes later, he barreled inside, his gaze finding her familiar, beloved face immediately. After so many horrible hours spent here, waiting to hear how his sister was doing or for news on his father's condition, this was the first time he'd ever entered a hospital giddy with anticipation. She was here! That had to be a good sign, didn't it? Maybe it had nothing to do with her feelings for him—after all, she hadn't told him she was applying for a job—but at least now he knew she'd be willing to live in the area and would never have to worry that he'd badgered her into it.

Although, once he'd caught up to her in Fort Worth, he'd been planning to badger, beg or seduce as necessary.

She walked over to him, her expression disbelieving. "I can't believe you were coming to see me."

"I can't believe you're *here*." Unable to stop himself, he lifted her into an off-the-ground hug and swung her around. "God, I've missed you."

She bit her lip, hesitating for an agonizing moment before admitting, "I've missed you, too."

Encouraged by his success so far, he decided to go for broke. "I love you, Sierra Bailey."

Her green eyes were huge, her expression stunned. "Wh-what?"

"I love you." Saying it out loud was amazingly liberating. He felt as if a crushing weight had been lifted off his chest. He took a deep breath, joy radiating through him.

"But I thought we were just a fling," she said.

He smoothed her hair away from her face. "No, that's what I needed to tell myself in order to let you go. I wasn't sure you could be happy here, or that you could love a—"

"I can! I do." She stood up on her tiptoes and he ducked his head, and they met each other in the middle for a kiss so hot he momentarily forgot where he was.

In her ear, he murmured, "I suppose it would be wrong for me to rip off your clothes in a hospital lobby? They have beds around here somewhere, right?"

She laughed, tugging his hand as she strode toward the exit. "My hotel is close." Suddenly, she stopped dead in her tracks. "You're sure? That you love me?"

"Positive." And he'd tell her over and over until it sank in. He recalled a piece of advice she'd given him once, regarding being a better brother. *Don't fall back on words alone. Be there for her.* He vowed to do exactly that. There were lots of romantic napkin notes in her future. He'd fill her life with slow dances and trail rides and stargazing and as much happiness as he could give her.

Her eyes shone with tears, but she tried to keep her voice light. "I only ask because I can be...challenging. I'm stubborn and bossy and independent."

"You mean determined and confident and strong?" He grinned down at her, looking forward to overcoming all the challenges they would face. Together. "I don't love you in spite of those things, darlin'. I love you because of them."

* * * * *

Read on for a sneak preview
of ONCE A RANCHER by
#1 New York Times *bestselling author*
Linda Lael Miller,
the first title in her brand-new series,
THE CARSONS OF MUSTANG CREEK.

CHAPTER ONE

SLATER CARSON WAS bone-tired, as he was after every film wrapped, but it was the best kind of fatigue—part pride and satisfaction in a job well done, part relief, part "bring it," that anticipatory quiver in the pit of his stomach that would lead him to the next project, and the one after that.

This latest film had been set in a particularly remote area, emphasizing how the Homestead Act had impacted the development of not just the American West, but the country as a whole. It had been his most ambitious effort to date. The sheer scope was truly epic, and as he watched the uncut footage on his computer monitor, he *knew*.

160 Acres was going to touch a nerve.

Yep. This one would definitely hit home with the viewers, new and old.

His previous effort, a miniseries on the Lincoln County War in New Mexico, had won prizes and garnered great reviews, and he'd sold the rights to one of the media giants for a shitload of money. Like *Lincoln County*, *160 Acres* was good, solid work. The researchers, camera operators and other professionals he worked with were the top people in the business, as committed to the films as he was.

And that was saying something.

No doubt about it, the team had done a stellar job the last time around, but this—well, *this* was the best yet. A virtual work of art, if he did say so himself.

"Boss?"

Slater leaned back in his desk chair and clicked the pause button. "Hey, Nate," he greeted his friend and personal assistant. "What do you need?"

Like Slater, Nate Wheaton had just gotten back from the film site, where he'd taken care of a thousand details, and it was a safe bet that the man was every bit as tired as he looked. Short, blond, energetic and not more than twenty years old, Nate was a dynamo; the production had come together almost seamlessly, in large part because of his talent, persistence and steel-trap brain.

"Um," Nate murmured, visibly unplugging, shifting gears. He was moving into off-duty mode, and God knew, he'd earned it. "There's someone to see you." He inclined his head in the direction of the outer office, rubbed the back of his neck and let out an exasperated sigh. "The lady insists she needs to talk to you and only you. I tried to get her to make an appointment, but she says it has to be now."

Slater suppressed a sigh of his own. "It's ten o'clock at night."

"I've actually pointed that out," Nate said, glancing at his phone. "It's five *after*, to be exact." Like Slater himself, Nate believed in exactness, which was at once a blessing and a curse. "She claims it can't possibly wait until morning, whatever 'it' is. But if I hadn't been walking into the kitchen I wouldn't have heard the knock."

"How'd she even find me?" The crew had flown

in late, driven out to the vineyard/ranch, and Slater had figured that no one, other than his family, knew he was in town. Or out of town. Whatever qualified as far as the ranch was concerned.

Nate looked glumly resigned. "I have no idea. She refused to say. I'm going to bed. If you need anything else, come and wake me, but bring a sledgehammer, because I'd probably sleep through anything less." A pause, another sigh, deeper and wearier than the last. "That was quite the shoot."

The understatement of the day.

Slater drew on the last dregs of his energy, shoved a hand through his hair and said, "Well, point her in this direction, if you don't mind, and then get yourself some shut-eye."

He supposed he sounded normal, but on the inside, he was drained. He'd given everything he had to *160 Acres*, and then some, and there was no hope of charging his batteries. He'd blown through the last of his physical resources hours ago.

Resentment at the intrusion nibbled at his famous equanimity; he was used to dealing with problems on the job—ranging from pesky all the way to apocalyptic— but at home, damn it, he expected to be left alone. He needed rest, downtime, a chance to regroup, and home was where he did those things.

One of his younger brothers ran the Carson ranch, and the other managed the vineyard and winery. The arrangement worked out pretty well. Everyone had his own role to play, and the sprawling mansion was big enough even for three competitive males to live in relative peace. Especially since Slater was gone half the time anyway.

"Will do." Nate left the study, and a few minutes later the door opened.

Before Slater could make the mental leap from one moment to the next, a woman—quite possibly the most beautiful woman he'd ever seen—stormed across the threshold, dragging a teenage boy by the arm.

She was a redhead, with the kind of body that would resurrect a dead man, let alone a tired one.

And Slater had a fondness for redheads; he'd dated a lot of them over the years. This one was all sizzle, and her riot of coppery curls, bouncing around her straight, indignant shoulders, seemed to blaze in the dim light.

It took him a moment, but he finally recovered enough to clamber to his feet and say, "I'm Slater Carson. Can I help you?"

This visitor, whoever she was, had his full attention.

Fascinating.

The redhead poked the kid, who was taller than she was by at least six inches, and she did it none too gently. The boy flinched; he was lanky, clad in a Seahawks T-shirt, baggy jeans and half-laced shoes. He looked bewildered, ready to bolt.

"Start talking, buster," the redhead ordered, glowering up at the kid. "And no excuses." She shook her head. "I'm being nice here," she said when the teenager didn't speak. "Your father would kick you into the next county."

Just his luck, Slater thought, with a strange, nostalgic detachment. She was married.

While he waited for the next development, he let his gaze trail over the goddess, over a sundress with thin straps on shapely shoulders, a midthigh skirt and a lot of silky, pale skin. She was one of the rare titian types who didn't have freckles, although Slater wouldn't be opposed to finding out if there might be a few tucked out of sight. White sandals with a small heel finished off the look, and all that glorious hair was loose and flowing down her back.

The kid, probably around fourteen, cleared his throat. He stepped forward and laid one of the magnetic panels from the company's production truck on the desk.

Slater, caught up in the unfolding drama, hadn't noticed the sign until then.

Interesting.

"I'm sorry," the boy gulped out, looking miserable and, at the same time, a little defiant. "I took this." He glanced briefly at the woman beside him, visibly considered giving her some lip, and just as visibly reconsidered. Smart kid. "I thought it was pretty cool," he explained, all knees and elbows and youthful angst. Color climbed his neck and burned in his face. "I know it was wrong, okay? Stealing is stealing, and my stepmother's ready to cuff me and haul me off to jail, so if that's what you want, too, mister, go for it."

Stepmother?

Slater was still rather dazed, as though he'd stepped off a wild carnival ride before it was through its whole slew of loop de loops.

"His father and I are divorced." She said it curtly, evidently reading Slater's expression.

Well, Slater reflected, that was good news. She did look young to be the kid's mother. And now that he thought about it, the boy didn't resemble her in the slightest, with his dark hair and eyes.

Finally catching up, he raised his brows, feeling a flicker of something he couldn't quite identify, along with a flash of sympathy for the boy. He guessed the redhead was in her early thirties. While she seemed to be in charge of the situation, Slater suspected she might be in over her head. Clearly, the kid was a handful.

It was time, Slater decided, still distanced from himself, to speak up.

"I appreciate your bringing it back," he managed, holding the boy's gaze but well aware of the woman on the periphery of his vision. "These aren't cheap."

Some of the F-you drained out of the kid's expression. "Like I said, I'm sorry. I shouldn't have done it."

"You made a mistake," Slater agreed quietly. "We've all done things we shouldn't have at one time or another. You did what you could to make it right, and that's good." He paused. "Life's all about the choices we make, son. Next time, try to do better." He felt a grin lurking at one corner of his mouth. "I would've been really ticked off if I had to replace this."

The boy looked confused. "Why? You're rich."

Slater had encountered that reasoning before—over the entire course of his life, actually. His family *was* wealthy, and had been for well over a century. They ran cattle, owned vast stretches of Wyoming grassland, and now, thanks to his mother's roots in the Napa Valley, there was the winery, with acres of vineyards to support the enterprise.

"Beside the point," Slater said. He worked for a living, and he worked hard, but he felt no particular need to explain that to this kid or anybody else. "What's your name?"

"Ryder," the boy answered after a moment's hesitation.

"Where do you go to school, Ryder?"

"The same lame place everyone around here goes in the eighth grade. Mustang Creek Middle School."

Slater lifted one hand. "I can do without the attitude," he said.

Ryder recovered quickly. "Sorry," he muttered.

Slater had never been married, but he understood children; he had a daughter, and he'd grown up with two kid brothers, born a year apart and still a riot looking for a place to happen, even in their thirties. He'd broken up more fights than a bouncer at Bad Billie's Biker Bar and Burger Palace on a Saturday night.

"I went to the same school," he said, mostly to keep the conversation going. He was in no hurry for the redhead to call it a night, especially since he didn't know her name yet. "Not a bad deal. Does Mr. Perkins still teach shop?"

Ryder laughed. "Oh, yeah. We call him 'The Relic.'"

Slater let the remark pass; it was flippant, but not mean-spirited. "You couldn't meet a nicer guy, though. Right?"

The kid's expression was suitably sheepish. "True," he admitted.

The stepmother glanced at Slater with some measure of approval, although she still seemed riled.

Slater looked back for the pure pleasure of it. She'd be a whole new experience, this one, and he'd never been afraid of a challenge.

She'd said she was divorced, which begged the question: What damn fool had let *her* get away?

As if she'd guessed what he was thinking—anybody

with her looks had to be used to male attention—the
redhead narrowed her eyes. Still, Slater thought he saw
a glimmer of amusement in them. She'd calmed down
considerably, but she wasn't missing a trick.

He grinned slightly. "Cuffs?" he inquired mildly,
remembering Ryder's statement a few minutes earlier.

She didn't smile, but that spark was still in her eyes.
"That was a reference to my former career," she replied, all business. "I'm an ex-cop." She put out her
hand, the motion almost abrupt, and finally introduced
herself. "Grace Emery," she said. "These days I run
the Bliss River Resort and Spa."

"Ah," Slater said, apropos of nothing in particular.
An ex-cop? Hot damn, she could handcuff him anytime. "You must be fairly new around here." If she
hadn't been, he would've made her acquaintance before now, or at least heard about her.

Grace nodded. Full of piss-and-vinegar moments
before, she looked tired now, and that did something
to Slater, although he couldn't have said exactly what
that something was. "It's a beautiful place," she said.
"Quite a change from Seattle." She stopped, looking
uncomfortable, maybe thinking she'd said too much.

Slater wanted to ask about the ex-husband, but the
time obviously wasn't right. He waited, sensing that
she might say more, despite the misgivings she'd just
revealed by clamming up.

Sure enough, she went on. "I'm afraid it's been
quite a change for Ryder, too." Another pause. "His
dad's military, and he's overseas. It's been hard on
him—Ryder, I mean."

Slater sympathized. The kid's father was out of the
country, he'd moved from a big city in one state to a

small town in another, and on top of that, he was fourteen, which was rough in and of itself. When Slater was that age, he'd grown eight inches in a single summer and simultaneously developed a consuming interest in girls without having a clue what to say to them. Oh, yeah. He remembered awkward.

He realized Grace's hand was still in his. He let go, albeit reluctantly.

Then, suddenly, he felt as tongue-tied as he ever had at fourteen. "My family's been on this ranch for generations," he heard himself say. "So I can't say I know what it would be like having to start over someplace new." *Shut up, man.* He couldn't seem to follow his own advice. "I travel a lot, and I'm always glad to get back to Mustang Creek."

Grace turned to Ryder, sighed, then looked back at Slater. "We've taken up enough of your time, Mr. Carson."

Mr. Carson?

"I'll walk you out," he said, still flustered and still trying to shake it off. Ordinarily, he was the proverbial man of few words, but tonight, in the presence of this woman, he was a babbling idiot. "This place is like a maze. I took over my father's office because of the view, but it's clear at the back of the house and—"

Had the woman *asked* for any of this information? No.

What the hell was the matter with him, anyway?

Grace didn't comment. The boy was already on the move, and she simply followed, which shot holes in Slater's theory about their ability to find their way to an exit without his guidance. He gave an internal shrug and trailed behind Grace, enjoying the gentle sway of her hips.

For some reason he wasn't a damn bit tired anymore.

Don't miss ONCE A RANCHER
by Linda Lael Miller,
available April 2016
wherever HQN books and ebooks are sold.

#1593 THE TEXAS RANGER'S FAMILY

Lone Star Lawmen • by Rebecca Winters

When Natalie Harris's ex-husband is killed, Kit Saunders is called in to investigate. The Texas Ranger quickly learns that Natalie and her sweet infant daughter are in danger...and he's the best man to protect them.

#1594 TWINS FOR THE BULL RIDER

Men of Raintree Ranch • by April Arrington

Champion bull rider Dominic Slade loves life on the road. But Cissy Henley and her rambunctious twin nephews need a man who'll stick around. Will he give up the thrill of the arena to be the father they need?

#1595 HER STUBBORN COWBOY

Hope, Montana • by Patricia Johns

When they were teens, Chet Granger destroyed Mackenzie Vaughn's relationship with his brother—or so she thought. But it turns out the noble rancher, now her next-door neighbor, may have had the best of intentions...

#1596 A MARRIAGE IN WYOMING

The Marshall Brothers • by Lynnette Kent

As a doctor, Rachel Vale believes in facts, not faith. Which is why there can be nothing between her and the town's cowboy minister, Garrett Marshall. The only problem is that Garrett believes the exact opposite...

REQUEST YOUR FREE BOOKS!
2 FREE NOVELS PLUS 2 FREE GIFTS!

H HARLEQUIN®

American Romance®

LOVE, HOME & HAPPINESS

YES! Please send me 2 FREE Harlequin® American Romance® novels and my 2 FREE gifts (gifts are worth about $10). After receiving them, if I don't wish to receive any more books, I can return the shipping statement marked "cancel." If I don't cancel, I will receive 4 brand-new novels every month and be billed just $4.74 per book in the U.S. or $5.49 per book in Canada. That's a savings of at least 12% off the cover price! It's quite a bargain! Shipping and handling is just 50¢ per book in the U.S. and 75¢ per book in Canada.* I understand that accepting the 2 free books and gifts places me under no obligation to buy anything. I can always return a shipment and cancel at any time. Even if I never buy another book, the two free books and gifts are mine to keep forever.

154/354 HDN GHZZ

Name	(PLEASE PRINT)

Address		Apt. #

City	State/Prov.	Zip/Postal Code

Signature (if under 18, a parent or guardian must sign)

Mail to the **Reader Service:**
IN U.S.A.: P.O. Box 1867, Buffalo, NY 14240-1867
IN CANADA: P.O. Box 609, Fort Erie, Ontario L2A 5X3

Want to try two free books from another line?
Call 1-800-873-8635 or visit www.ReaderService.com.

* Terms and prices subject to change without notice. Prices do not include applicable taxes. Sales tax applicable in N.Y. Canadian residents will be charged applicable taxes. Offer not valid in Quebec. This offer is limited to one order per household. Not valid for current subscribers to Harlequin American Romance books. All orders subject to credit approval. Credit or debit balances in a customer's account(s) may be offset by any other outstanding balance owed by or to the customer. Please allow 4 to 6 weeks for delivery. Offer available while quantities last.

Your Privacy—The Reader Service is committed to protecting your privacy. Our Privacy Policy is available online at www.ReaderService.com or upon request from the Reader Service.

We make a portion of our mailing list available to reputable third parties that offer products we believe may interest you. If you prefer that we not exchange your name with third parties, or if you wish to clarify or modify your communication preferences, please visit us at www.ReaderService.com/consumerschoice or write to us at Reader Service Preference Service, P.O. Box 9062, Buffalo, NY 14240-9062. Include your complete name and address.

HAR15

*When Natalie Harris's ex-husband is killed,
Miles "Kit" Saunders is called in to investigate.
The Texas Ranger quickly learns that Natalie, and her
sweet infant daughter, are in danger...and he's the best
man to protect them.*

Read on for a sneak peek of
THE TEXAS RANGER'S FAMILY
by Rebecca Winters, the third book in her
LONE STAR LAWMEN *miniseries.*

"Mrs. Harris?"

Whatever picture of the Ranger Natalie may have had in her mind didn't come close to the sight of the tall, thirtyish, hard-muscled male in a Western shirt, jeans and cowboy boots.

Her gaze flitted over his dark brown hair only to collide with his beautiful hazel eyes appraising her through a dark fringe of lashes.

"I'm Miles Saunders." She felt the stranger's probing look pierce her before he showed her his credentials. That was when she noticed the star on his shirt pocket.

This man is the real thing. The stuff that made the Texas Rangers legendary. She had the strange feeling that she'd seen him somewhere before, but shrugged it off. This was definitely the first time she'd ever met a Ranger.

"Come in." Her voice faltered, mystified by this unexpected visit. She was pretty sure the Rangers didn't investigate a home break-in.

"Thank you." He took a few steps on those long, powerful legs. His presence dominated the kitchen. She invited him to follow her into the living room.

"Please sit down." She indicated the upholstered chair on the other side of the coffee table while she took the matching chair. There was no place else to sit until the destroyed room was put back together.

He did as she asked. "I understand you have a daughter. Is she here?"

The man already knew quite a bit about her, she realized. "No. I left her with my sitter."

He studied one of the framed photos that hadn't been knocked off the end table, even though a drawer had been pulled out. "She looks a lot like you, especially the eyes. She's a little beauty."

Natalie looked quickly at the floor, stunned by the personal comment. He'd sounded sincere. So far everything about him surprised her so much she couldn't think clearly.

He turned to focus his attention on Natalie. "You're very composed for someone who's been through so much."

"I'm trying to hold it together." After all, with her own personal Texas Ranger guarding her and Amy day and night, what was there to be worried about?

Don't miss THE TEXAS RANGER'S FAMILY by Rebecca Winters, available May 2016 wherever Harlequin® American Romance® books and ebooks are sold.

www.Harlequin.com

HAREXP0416